So far as I can see now, there is nothing wrong with these rejected
characters, no reason these scenes would not have read as well
as any that appear in the final version. I never of my own
free will, rejected them. T~~~~~~~~~~~~~~~~~~~~~~~~~~~~racters
of the novel who, at a certa~~~~~~~~~~~~~~~~~~~~~~~~~~the fourth
~~and final draft~~, took over, ~~~~~~~~~~~~~~~~~~~~~~~~determin~
their own actions, and decid~~~~~~~~~~~~~~~~~~~~~~~~~the novel
must follow. ~~It~~ This is, I suspect, the common experience of most novel~
The odd ~~xxxxxxxx~~ only thing is that none of this material can ever be
~~d in any other piece of writing~~. These rejected scenes and
~~ch~~racters all owe their exitence to ~~a single situation, covered~~ the story they were a part of
the fact that, ~~~~~~~~~~~~~~~~ This story ~~~~~ des covered
~~~~~~~~~ final shaping of ~~it~~ they were reveal~~~~

To waken on a winter morning on that island was not to fi~
you would here, darkness and cold everywhere outside the wa~
bed. ~~In~~ That part of the world is never cold. It rains harder t~
any rain you ~~have~~ ever seen, ~~and~~ Sometimes it rains for months, But it never snows
~~people who live there have never seen snow~~. At nig t there are were
of the same stars that you ~~knew~~ see, for example, but not all of them, and they w~
hard to recognize---the handle of the ~~Big~~ Dipper never rose above
~~so how can you tell was the Big Dipper~~ now they were ~~and you can't~~
the northern horizon---~~because they were mixed in with so many~~
the sky over
thousands of stars that are never seen in ~~Xxxxxxxxxxxxxxxx~~ the Uni~
States. ~~The cup of the Big Dipper was there, but the handle never~~
rose above the northern horizon, so how could you tell it was the
~~Big Dipper~~ There were are people on the island, and animals, and bir~
and lizards, ~~and~~ insects, trees, grass, and huge flowers as big as
your face. ~~In~~ the springtime the trees broke out into flowers. The~
were mountains and clouds and sometimes a rainbow. ~~~~~~
and villages, and ~~~~~~~~~~~~~~~~~~~~~~~~
~~~~~~~~~~~ and the farms ~~~~~ called plantations
~~~~~~~~ people didn't say "Good morning," or "Good evening~
~~~~~~ said "Bon jour" and "Bonne Nuit" ~~~~~~
island belo~~~~~

PRAISE FOR WILLIAM MAXWELL

"William Maxwell never indulges in writing for writing's sake. Rather he puts together exquisite sentences propelled by his search for understanding. Although Maxwell tells us that his writing process involves revision after revision, his prose is simple and direct. It flows as if it came into being without artifice, without struggle. He talks to you. His quiet voice is close by. You can imagine sitting by a fire while Maxwell answers your questions about how he became a writer or how an autobiographical fiction writer writes. He keeps a slight distance, a light touch. Thanks to this gentlemanly reserve, what he says is intimate without ever becoming cloying. He does not tell you more than what you want to know. As his stories unfold, you can picture his gentle smile. If he had a dimple, it would deepen."

—HAYDEN HERRERA, author of *Upper Bohemia*

"It is not William Maxwell's narratives or the characters, tenderly imagined as they are, that draw me back, so much as his creation of an American Midwest. It is a Midwest set in time, and yet timeless, haunted in a way that makes nostalgia impossible. That haunted sense is a gift he shares with Sherwood Anderson. Maxwell's voice and the subtly of his prose are his alone. His work is rightly described as spare, but spare does not convey its signature purity. One is made aware not simply of its beautiful cadence, but also the silence surrounding the cadence."

—STUART DYBEK, author of
Ecstatic Cahoots: Fifty Short Stories

THE WRITER AS ILLUSIONIST

THE WRITER
AS ILLUSIONIST

UNCOLLECTED & UNPUBLISHED WORK

William Maxwell

SELECTED AND INTRODUCED BY
ALEC WILKINSON

BOSTON
GODINE NONPAREIL
2024

Published in 2024 by
GODINE
Boston, Massachusetts
godine.com

LIBRARY OF CONGRESS CATALOGING-IN-PUBLICATION DATA
Names: Maxwell, William, 1908-2000, author. | Wilkinson, Alec, 1952-
    editor, writer of introduction.
Title: The writer as illusionist : uncollected & unpublished work / William
    Maxwell ; selected and introduced by Alec Wilkinson.
Other titles: Writer as illusionist (Compilation)
Description: Boston : Godine, 2023.
Identifiers: LCCN 2023005387 (print) | LCCN 2023005388 (ebook) | ISBN
    9781567927962 (hardcover) | ISBN 9781567927979 (ebook)
Subjects: LCSH: Maxwell, William, 1908-2000. | Maxwell, William,
    1908-2000--Friends and associates. | Authorship. | LCGFT:
    Autobiographies. | Diaries. | Literary criticism. | Essays.
Classification: LCC PS3525.A9464 Z46 2023 (print) | LCC PS3525.A9464
    (ebook) | DDC 813/.54 [B]--dc23/eng/20230329
LC record available at https://lccn.loc.gov/2023005387
LC ebook record available at https://lccn.loc.gov/2023005388

First Printing, 2024
Printed in the United States of America

For
M. C.
C. B.
and
E. H.

CONTENTS

Introduction

SOME OF THE writing in this book originally appeared in *The New Yorker*, the first piece in 1937, when William Maxwell was twenty-eight, and the last piece in 1998, when Maxwell was eighty-nine. One piece was printed in *The New York Times*; three pieces were published as prefaces to collections of Maxwell's writing; and one piece, a speech given at Smith College in 1955, was published in *A William Maxwell Portrait*, a book of reminiscences of Maxwell organized by the poets Edward Hirsch and Michael Collier and the novelist Charles Baxter a few years after Maxwell died in 2000. Much of the writing, however, has not been printed before. The unpublished material is from several sources. There are selections from a journal that Maxwell kept in New Mexico in 1940, when he was in his early thirties, and, feeling that he had been overlooked for a promotion, had quit his job as an

editor at *The New Yorker* and driven to New Mexico with
a friend. He stayed five weeks and came home thinking
that he might have sufficient material for a novel. Instead
he used parts of what he had written in *The Folded Leaf*,
which was published in 1945. I have placed these entries
in a section that also includes an account of Maxwell's
moving as a young man from Illinois to New York and
being hired by *The New Yorker*. This material comes from
a letter he wrote me. He wrote me the letter and gave me
the New Mexico pieces when I was writing a profile of
him for *The New Yorker* in 1999. The rest of the unpublished material I found in files after he died, which his
daughter Kate gave me permission to read through. (The
Maxwells' younger daughter, Brooke, an artist and social
activist, died of cancer in 2015, at fifty-nine.) The book
ends with writing about himself and his family and their
lives in New York, and this writing is from those files.

Maxwell was a species of autobiographical writer but
he wasn't a confessional one. The difference, as I see it, is
that while both types of writers may be motivated by the
desire to shed an emotional burden, a confessional writer
candidly reveals the facts of his or her life or their life,
as if handing over the keys of one's house to the reader.
For a confessional writer to conceal is to mislead. Also,
in confessional writing—straight autobiography, that is—
the narrator and the writer are the same person, and the
record itself is the text. An autobiographical writer, at least
as Maxwell defined one, examines the past for patterns
and meaning, might withhold a great deal, and resembles,
perhaps, but is usually not strictly the person in the text.

I raise this to point out that as often as Maxwell wrote about things that actually happened to him—about his childhood in Illinois, and the death of his mother in the influenza epidemic of 1918–1919—he wasn't given to revealing himself or the lives of people he knew beyond what his art entailed. He cared sufficiently about other people's feelings that he never permitted *The Chateau*, which was a bestseller in America, to be published in France because he was concerned that some of the French characters, among them the owner of the chateau, might be offended by how they were portrayed. In his private writing he considered story ideas involving people he knew and decided not to pursue the ideas because they might lead to someone he cared about feeling exposed.

It was something of a surprise to me to find that Maxwell in his private writing was less guarded than I knew him to be. I had thought that the way I knew him was the way that he always was. I don't know why I clung to such an innocent notion, but I did. In any case, the tone of the private writing is more intimate and confiding than even his letters were. Letter writing is a dialogue, of course, and journal writing is too, if only a dialogue with different sides of oneself. It is not uncommon to keep alive within us people we loved who are dead, their manners and habits and ways of speaking, and to feel that they are accessible to us. A few days before Maxwell died I said what I had been trying not to say, which was, "How will I ever do without you?" and he said, "You won't have to, because I won't ever leave you." Somewhere in an interview Maxwell gave when he was an elderly man, which Michael

Collier made me aware of, Maxwell says that he wrote his books for his mother. Reading his private writing I feel that the person he is addressing might seem to be her, that he is making her aware of what his life has consisted of and how it is unfolding, and that he is telling her stories. I don't mean that I think this is a conscious intention, only that it seems present in a shadow way among his purposes.

Maxwell was not an easy person to talk to—at least I didn't find him to be. He was reserved in a way that I think of as typically midwestern, at least typical of midwesterners of his generation. Also, he tended to think carefully before he spoke, so there were longer pauses than is usual in conversation. In addition, he had a tendency toward an indirection of a literal kind. Several years before he died, driving in a rainstorm, he turned across the path of a car he hadn't seen until it was too late. While being deposed by the other driver's lawyer, he was asked how long was the interval between his seeing the car and the crash. Maxwell hesitated, then said, "I told myself, you must accept whatever happens." The lawyer became indignant, because he thought that Maxwell was being evasive and was perhaps even senile. Maxwell, though, had given a precise answer. From the moment he saw the other car to when the crash happened he had time for a single thought.

I never knew him to be in a rush to express himself or to impose his opinions. It occurs to me that I never once heard him argue, although it isn't possible that he agreed with everything he heard. He had favored Adlai Stevenson's candidacy in 1952, and my mother had been for Eisenhower. He spent election night at my parents' house, listening to the radio, and when it was announced that Stevenson had lost he began drinking so that he could say unacceptable things and not be blamed. He shocked my mother and left that night thinking that he wouldn't ever be invited back. That is the only occasion of misbehavior that I am aware of. When Maxwell was first at *The New Yorker*, one of the other editors used to take him to lunch to hear gossip, and when the editor realized that Maxwell wasn't going to talk about the other people in the office, the editor stopped inviting him.

When I was young I thought that the world was made up of great men and women, the pattern of whose lives I might emulate. Some of these people I knew—Maxwell, William Shawn, Joseph Mitchell—and some I knew through their books—Mark Twain, Isak Dinesen, Hemingway, Rebecca West, and Sybille Bedford. Chekhov. Bruce Chatwin. Ralph Ellison and Zora Neale Hurston. Writers. It didn't occur to me that there was something one could do more exalted than writing. I didn't begin writing until I was twenty-four, and I had a convert's zeal. I have lived long enough now to see Maxwell more entirely than I saw him when I was young. I'm not sure we would have been friends if we had been the same age. He was recessive, and I liked more boisterous companions. When he was alive, I tended to see him as not having any flaws. I see him now as capable of mistakes and misjudgments, more complete, but still deeply alluring and original. My regard for his writing, for what he managed to dramatize, has only grown. He believed that writing, and especially autobiographical writing, requires that the writer have a god's-eye view, so that experiences that are entirely personal reverberate in such a way that they move a disinterested reader. When I read *So Long, See You Tomorrow*, of which this objectivity is a hallmark, or the pieces here, "Nearing Ninety" or "The Room Outside," or the prefaces or nearly any of the other work, I am still often amazed—at the subtlety of the art, the depth of what he saw, the intricate connections, at his capacity for dramatizing situations that require a rare hand and eye. "Pay attention," he often told me, especially when I was about to enter a situation that was complicated and difficult.

Maxwell not infrequently said, to me and to others, that he never kept a journal, that anything worth writing about was something a writer would remember. This, it turns out, was disingenuous, and I have no idea why he said it. The questions one might ask of the dead pile up, and it is, after all, only one question I might ask him. He said it when he was an old man, and he may have meant that he had come to believe it to be true, although he hadn't always believed it. Anyway, Maxwell's diary keeping was very episodic. So far as I can tell, years sometimes passed between entries, decades even. He seemed to write things down when he was young and when he was middle-aged but not to do it as an elderly man. The Maxwells lived in Manhattan but they had a small house in the country not far from the city. Maxwell had moved into the house in the nineteen forties before he was married. It was a cottage that had been delivered to its acre of land on a flatbed truck, and he had written nearly all of his stories and novels there. For a while when he was young and before he was married he had a housekeeper who disapproved of his reading and writing all day, as if they weren't proper ways for a man to spend his time. For years the Maxwells spent every weekend at the house and sometimes the whole summer, but toward the end of their lives one difficulty or another intervened and they went to the house less and less often. They let my wife and son and me use it, and for several years we went practically every weekend, often with their daughter Kate. Opening a drawer one day in the room where Maxwell worked, I found a small notebook in which he had kept ideas for stories. For a few years after he and his wife were married, they had lived in the house. They moved to the city when their daughters were old enough to go to school. Maxwell had kept this record while riding on the train back and forth to his office in the city. If I had known I wouldn't be able to find it after he died, I would have kept it. I'm sorry I didn't, because it's lost now.

Since I thought I could account for pretty much all the periods when Maxwell was at work on something, it did not occur to me that he also had periods when he was without a piece of writing to work on. All artists have fallow periods, I just didn't think that he did. It was a surprise to me, then, to find in his files the folder of story ideas that are published here. I have always liked reading the notebook that Chekhov kept of ideas for stories and plays. In recording remarks from a Russian dinner party or describing someone he saw in the street or a love affair, he seems present in a way that he doesn't otherwise on the page, and for the same reason it pleases me to reproduce some of Maxwell's entries. They portray the mind of an artist seeking a way into the interior life, trying this door and that, seeing which one might open and where it might lead.

My plan for assembling the material might not appear obvious, so perhaps it would be helpful if I described how I have put it together. In the loosest sense I followed the chronology of Maxwell's life. I say loosest because it wasn't possible to stick to it strictly, at least if I believed that there was an inherent emotional structure to some of the entries or that some of them could be placed more aptly together regardless of when they happened. What I hoped to achieve was to make Maxwell seem present so that a reader might feel that he or she or they had met him.

In Part I, Maxwell describes his childhood and growing up, being with his mother and father, his becoming a writer, his moving to New York and being hired by *The New Yorker* and taught to be an editor. He was twenty-eight when he was hired, and he spent nearly all of the following forty years at the magazine, first in the Art and then in the Fiction departments. He left twice that I know of, once in the fit of pique for New Mexico, and once in the hope, before it got too late, of establishing himself as a writer. Sometimes the material from New Mexico went almost untouched from the journal into the novel, and other times it was reworked. At a ceremony held in 1998 to celebrate Maxwell's fifty years as a member of a club for artists and writers in New York, several people read excerpts from Maxwell's work. Roger

Angell read the passage from *So Long, See You Tomorrow* in which Maxwell walks each evening with his father through the downstairs rooms of the house, with his arm around his father's waist, in the year after his mother has died, and Maxwell is ten years old.

Shirley Hazzard read a passage from *The Folded Leaf* that describes the stages of taking a journey and what a traveler experiences, and when I found, years later, after both Maxwell and Hazzard were dead, the entries in Maxwell's files that pertained to this period, I realized where the passage had come from. There are, of course, other examples of writers using material from journals in their work, some of them probably famous, but I am not aware of them, and I hope that Maxwell's use of such material will be as interesting to other readers as it is to me. To me it suggests, in the writing of fiction, something of the collage-like interplay among observation of the present, the imaginative life, and the pull of memory.

After the summer in New Mexico, Maxwell went back to New York and *The New Yorker*. The preface to his essay collection *The Outermost Dream* describes 1948 and the ways in which in the early days of *The New Yorker* people did different tasks. Maxwell occasionally wrote stories for Talk of the Town. A short selection of these is followed by two pieces from the magazine about islands—Martinique, where Maxwell had gone as a young man, and Bermuda. The piece about Bermuda is the only long piece of reporting that Maxwell ever wrote. He might have written more of them, since such pieces paid well, but this one was edited by William Shawn, who wasn't yet the editor that he became, and Maxwell so disliked the way that Shawn handled his text that he made up his mind not to let himself fall into Shawn's hands again.

More than thirty years later, in 1976, when Maxwell retired from *The New Yorker*, Shawn wrote him a letter in which he said, "Perhaps no one has ever known more about the writing of fiction." Part II includes remarks Maxwell made about writing, some of them in a speech, but most of them private. This section also includes things he said on accepting various awards and ideas he had for stories and novels that for the most part never got written. Maxwell's novel *The Folded Leaf* concerns the intimate adolescent friendship of two boys, Spud Latham and Lymie Peters. Maxwell thought that writing about adolescents involved difficulties different from those involved in writing about grown-up men and women, and this section includes some of his thoughts on the matter.

Part III includes a piece from *The New Yorker* about the letters of Robert Louis Stevenson, a writer Maxwell had admired since reading *Treasure Island* as a boy; tributes to other artists, sometimes in the form of obituary and memorial notices; a speech on the subject of writing and writers; and the preface to an edition of three novels—*Time Will Darken It, The Chateau, So Long, See You Tomorrow*—that turns attention toward Maxwell's private life.

Part IV includes selections from Maxwell's private journals, writing, that is, about his family and himself. It ends with a reminiscence from *The New Yorker*, published in 1998, which was the last piece he wrote for the magazine. The last piece the magazine published, in 1999, a story called "Grape Bay" that takes place in Bermuda, had been written years earlier, and Maxwell found it among his files as he was organizing his papers.

Alec Wilkinson
New York, 2023

THE WRITER AS ILLUSIONIST

PART I

CHILDHOOD, EARLY YEARS

Nearing Ninety
New York Times, 1997

OUT OF THE corner of my eye I see my 90th birthday approaching. It is one year and six months away. How long after that will I be the person I am now?

I don't yet need a cane but I have a feeling that my table manners have deteriorated. My posture is what you'd expect of someone addicted to sitting in front of a typewriter, but it was always that way. "Stand up straight," my father would say. "You're all bent over like an old man." It didn't bother me then and it doesn't now, though I agree that an erect carriage is a pleasure to see, in someone of any age.

I have regrets but there are not very many of them and, fortunately, I forget what they are. I forget names too, but it is not yet serious. What I am trying to remember and can't, quite often my wife will remember. And vice versa. She is in and out during the day but I know she will be home when evening comes, and so I am never lonely. Long ago, a neighbor in the country, looking at our flower garden, said, "Children and roses reflect their care." This is true of the very old as well.

I am not—I think I am not—afraid of dying. When I was seventeen I worked on a farm in southern Wisconsin, near Portage. It was no ordinary farm and not much serious farming was done there, but it had the look of a place

5

that had been lived in, and loved, for a good long time. The farm had come down in that family through several generations, to a woman who was so alive that everything and everybody seemed to revolve around her personality. She lived well into her nineties and then one day told her oldest daughter that she didn't want to live anymore, that she was tired. This remark reconciled me to my own inevitable extinction. I could believe that enough is enough.

Because I actively enjoy sleeping, dreams, the unexplainable dialogues that take place in my head as I am drifting off, all that, I tell myself that lying down to an afternoon nap that goes on and on through eternity is not something to be concerned about. What spoils this pleasant fancy is the recollection that when people are dead they don't read books. This I find unbearable. No Tolstoy, no Chekhov, no Elizabeth Bowen, no Keats, no Rilke. One might as well be—

Before I am ready to call it quits I would like to reread every book I have ever deeply enjoyed, beginning with Jane Austen and going through shelf after shelf of the bookcases, until I arrive at the "Autobiographies" of William Butler Yeats. As it is, I read a great deal of the time. I am harder to please, though. I see flaws in masterpieces. Conrad indulging in rhetoric when he would do better to get on with it. I would read all day long and well into the night if there were no other claims on my time. Appointments with doctors, with the dentist. The monthly bank statement. Income tax returns. And because I don't want to turn into a monster, people. Afternoon tea with X, dinner with the Y's. Our social life would be a good deal more active than it is if more than half of those I care about hadn't passed over to the other side.

I did not wholly escape the amnesia that overtakes children around the age of six but I carried along with me more of my childhood than, I think, most people do. Once, after dinner, my father hitched up the horse and took my mother and me for a sleigh ride. The winter stars were very bright. The sleigh bells made a lovely sound. I was bundled up to the nose, between my father and mother, where nothing, not even the cold, could get at me. The very perfection of happiness.

At something like the same age, I went for a ride, again with my father and mother, on a riverboat at Havana, Illinois. It was a side-wheeler and the decks were screened, I suppose as protection against the mosquitoes. Across eight decades the name of the steamboat comes back to me—the Eastland—bringing with it the context of disaster. A year later, at the dock in Chicago, too many of the passengers crowded on one side, waving goodbye, and it rolled over and sank. Trapped by the screens everywhere, a great many people lost their lives. The fact that I had been on this very steamboat, that I had escaped from a watery grave, I continued to remember all through my childhood.

I have liked remembering almost as much as I have liked living. But now it is different, I have to be careful. I can ruin a night's sleep by suddenly, in the dark, thinking about some particular time in my life. Before I can stop myself it is as if I had driven a mine shaft down through layers and layers of the past and must explore, relive, remember, reconsider, until daylight delivers me.

I have not forgotten the pleasure, when our children were very young, of hoisting them onto my shoulders when their legs gave out. Of reading to them at bedtime. Of studying their beautiful faces. But that was more than thirty years ago. I admire the way that, as adults, they have taken hold of life, and I am glad that they are not materialistic, but there is little or nothing I can do for them at this point, except write a little fable to put in their Christmas stocking.

"Are you writing?" people ask—out of politeness, undoubtedly. And I say, "Nothing very much." The truth but not the whole truth—which is that I seem to have lost touch with the place that stories and novels come from. I have no idea why. I still like making sentences.

Every now and then, in my waking moments, and especially when I am in the country, I stand and look hard at everything.

Preface to *All the Days and Nights*, Maxwell's collected stories, published in 1994.

THE FOUR-MASTED SCHOONER lay at anchor in Gravesend Bay, not far from Coney Island. It belonged to J. P. Morgan, and I persuaded a man with a rowboat to take me out to it. In my coat pocket was a letter of introduction to the captain. The year was 1933, and I was twenty-five. I had started to become an English professor and changed my mind, and I had written a novel, as yet unpublished. I meant to go to sea, so that I would have something to write about. And because I was under the impression, gathered from the dust-jacket copy of various best-sellers that it was something a writer did before he settled down and devoted his life to writing. While the captain was reading my letter I looked around. The crew consisted of one sailor, chipping rust, with a police dog at his side. It turned out that the schooner had been there for four years because Mr. Morgan couldn't afford to use it. The captain was tired of doing nothing and was expecting a replacement the next day and was therefore not in a position to take me on. He had no idea when the beautiful tall-masted ship would leave its berth. And I had no idea that three-quarters of the material I would need for the rest of my writing life was already at my disposal. My father and mother. My brothers. The cast of larger-than-life-size characters—affectionate aunts, friends of the family, neighbors white and black—that I was presented with when I came into the world. The look of things. The weather. Men and women long at rest in the cemetery but vividly remembered. The Natural History of home: the suede glove on the front-hall table, the unfinished game of solitaire, the oriole's nest suspended from the tip of the outermost branch of the elm tree, dandelions in the grass. All there, waiting for me to learn my trade and recognize instinctively what would make a story or sustain the complicated cross-weaving of longer fiction.

I think it is generally agreed that stories read better one at a time. They need air around them. And they need thinking about, since they tend to have both an explicit and an un-spelled-out meaning. Inevitably, some of the stories I wrote, especially when I was young, are stuck fast in their period—or to put it differently, the material was not as substantial as it ought to have been—and I see no reason to republish them. When I was working on the ninth version of "A Final Report" I came on the seventh in a desk drawer, and saw that it was better than the one I was working on and that I must have been too tired when I finished it to realize that there was no need to pursue the idea any further. On the other hand, "Love" came right the first time, without a word having to be changed and I thought—mistakenly—that I had had a breakthrough, and stories would be easier to write from that moment on; all I needed to do was just *say* it.

The stories I have called "improvisations" really are that. They were written for an occasion—for a birthday or to be rolled up inside a red ribbon and inserted among the ornaments on the Christmas tree. I wrote them to please my wife, over a great many years. When we were first married, after we had gone to bed I would tell her a story in the dark. They came from I had no idea where. Sometimes I fell asleep in the middle of a story and she would shake me and say "What happened next?" and I would struggle up through layers of oblivion and tell her.

A biographical sketch, from Maxwell's files, unpublished.

I WAS BORN in the small, central-Illinois town of Lincoln, on August 16, 1908. There were lawyers on both sides of the family and when I was old enough to listen to the conversation of my elders, I found that it was often about legal battles involving lost wills and the inheritance of so many acres of Illinois land. All around the town the land lay, rich and black and flat and fertile, and the sky over it like an inverted bowl. I saw the end of wagons and buggies and sleighs, and the pulling down of back-yard barns to make room for garages. My mother died in the influenza epidemic of 1918-19. I have two brothers, both lawyers. My father was in the insurance business. When I was 15, we moved to Chicago and the change from a small town to the city, from a small high school to a school of 3000 was so great that no sink or swim social experience has ever been as serious or as stimulat-ing. In Lincoln I had had daydreams of going to some other place, where nobody knew me, and changing from an introspective unconfident boy, good at studies but bad at games, into a happy outgoing athlete. The change did not occur, needless to say, and the knowledge that there are areas in which people do not and cannot change—do not even want to change, because they are what they are because they are also a recognizable human type (the writer of prose fiction is one) did not come until a long time afterward.

In the summers I worked for my father in an insurance office in the Loop, doing clerical work, and there were two things outside that. I became addicted to the opera which was performed all summer long at Ravinia park, and for years I stood through the standard repertory, at the back of the shell. I also became obsessed with Lake

Michigan, which lay a few blocks to the east of where we lived. It was not enough to spend Saturday afternoon and Sunday there. I began getting up and going to the lake before breakfast, and then before daylight. These two, the operas and the great body of water, hung over my mind for years.

From a journal.

After graduating from the University of Illinois, Maxwell went to graduate school at Harvard on a scholarship from the Harvard Club of Chicago.

I STAYED AT Harvard only one year, but that was a rich and happy one. I lived in a Victorian dormitory not under the control of the university, without another undergraduate or graduate student. The corridors were half empty, and inhabited largely by old women. The ceilings were high, there was no electricity, the bathtub was tin, there was a window seat overlooking a park. I worked six hours a day on German alone, having acquired a psychological block against that language from, I suppose, having been a little boy during the First World War. I memorized all of "Dichtung und Wahrheit," "Goetz von Berlichengen," "Tasso," and "Iphegenie" *in English*, in order to be able to translate passages from them at sight. A very kind understanding professor named Waltz kept me from sinking entirely out of sight, but could not in all fairness give me a better grade than B, which was not enough for my graduate scholarship to be renewed. At Harvard I met Robert Fitzgerald and James Agee, and took a course under Theodore Spencer. Fitzgerald enriched my mind, changed my character, and set me to writing prose instead of poetry.

A childhood memory, from a journal.

I WAS BROUGHT up to believe that my father had never laid his hand on me. "Happy yes," he used to say. "He was full of the Old Ned. But you were very different. There was no need to punish you." I took his word for it, and felt somehow underprivileged. The statement was not true, though it was what he sincerely believed. In the last year of his very long life he was presented with something from the underground vaults: a Sunday morning in the year 1911. I was three years old. My mother had dressed me all in white to go to dinner at my grandfather's house, and as we were crossing the street, my father saw me heading straight for a mud puddle and said, "Bill, if you walk through that mud puddle, I'll take you upstairs and spank you." I did walk through it, and he was a man who believed in keeping his word.

I look forward very much to this aspect of old age—to lost scenes that will be restored to me in all their original freshness, and the clearing up of God knows what mistakes and uncertainties. The things I suddenly remember now, at fifty-nine, are not from this far down; that is, I remember that I have remembered them before, at intervals, and then forgotten them. And will again. The memory itself is not always very interesting, but if I stop and gather in all the strands that are attached to it, it is worth examining. Yesterday afternoon I had to transact by telephone some business of a highly detailed sort that called for accuracy and judgment at every moment, and the call went on for two hours and 15 minutes. I had not slept well the night before and had had a taxing day, and from time to time during the last forty-five minutes of the call I would glance at the clock on the wall of my office and then at the thickness of the pile of sheets that remained to be dealt with. And several times a feeling of weakness, bordering on nausea, came over me and I wasn't sure I was going to make it—to finish what had to be done, and done right then. And suddenly I remembered being in a rowboat with my father and mother, on the Illinois River. I was perhaps a year or two older than I was that Sunday morning. Old enough, in any case, to perceive what I wouldn't have perceived at three. They had gone fishing, downstream from the resort we were staying in, and had taken me with them. We were at a place where the river widened out to become a lake, and one of those sudden Illinois thunderstorms had blown up, out of the heat and heaviness of the August afternoon. The sky was black, and there were whitecaps. And my father was rowing steadily and hard toward the hotel landing, out of sight, around a bend in the river. I liked storms, and was not afraid of thunder and lightning. I was enjoying the wind and the peculiar light and all that excitement in the sky, until my father said, "Bill, get down in the bottom of the boat." In his voice I heard that he was afraid—a thing I didn't know could happen! I did as he told me, and then looked at my mother for enlightenment. *You know I trust your father absolutely but we're in trouble* is what I read in her face, *and it isn't his fault or anybody's, but we shouldn't be out here on the river, in a storm like this, in a rowboat. Stay still as you can* . . . Though I weighed no more than a feather, they were both heavy people, my mother especially, and the stern of the rowboat sat low in the water. I can hear the creaking of the oarlocks, across half a century. The air has turned fresh, the way it does just before the rain comes. My father is doing the best he can, but if the storm breaks while we are still out in this boat, what will become of us?

From *Ancestors: A Family History* (1971).

What brought Maxwell's childhood to an end was the death of his mother.

WHAT I CAN remember of my childhood (which came to an end at that moment) all lies in the framework of seven or eight years, during which I was much more aware of the seasons than I was of the calendar, though I made several of them in school and brought them home to my mother to use. Sometimes it seems as if everything happened in a single long day that can be unwound inch by inch like a Chinese scroll. And I do not so much remember things as see them happening. In much the same way that my Aunt Bert saw Mary Edie setting out with a baby in her arms to find her husband, I see a man and a woman—both young, in their early thirties—and a little boy, fishing on the Illinois river. The river is very wide at this point, and the man does not like the look of the sky. He puts his fishing pole away and begins to row. The oarlocks creak in a slow steady rhythm. The rowboat sits low in the water. The resort where they are staying is a long way, around a bend in the river. The wind is blowing now, and the sky is getting blacker and blacker. *Creak. Creak. Creak.* The air is green. The sky is split open by forked lightning and this is followed by a massive clap of thunder. There are white-caps on the water. When the man tells the little boy to get down in the bottom of the boat, the little boy hears in his voice that his father is afraid. He turns and looks at his mother, in the stern of the boat. She, too. The little boy now knows something he didn't know before: It isn't true that nothing bad can happen to them. The knowledge is remote as, lying in bed at home, he smells the snow that has fallen in the night. But it is nevertheless permanent.

Beginnings.

The first piece of writing that Maxwell ever pub-lished was a short story about an aristocrat who hid in a grandfather's clock, during the French Revo-lution. He was fourteen at the time, and living in Lincoln "where there were any number of very interesting people," he wrote in a journal, "but no-body who was in any way connected with the *ancien régime*, and so I think the story must've been derived from literary sources."

The summer Maxwell was sixteen, he spent in Wisconsin as a house boy at a lake club at Oconomowoc where he had gone with his friend Jack Scully, from whom the character Spud Latham in *The Folded Leaf* is drawn. The next summer Maxwell worked on the farm near Portage. "People came there, musicians and writers, from as far away as New York, and I was taken to meet the writer Zona Gale," he wrote. "I could no more pin her down, say what she really was, or who, than any of the other young writers she helped and encouraged and started on their careers. She was something rare and wonderful. She was, for me, so far as I was concerned, the Phoenix. She was also a much finer writer than is now generally realized." Gale was the first woman to win the Pulitzer Prize for Drama, in 1921.

As a small boy, "perhaps from watching my mother pursue china painting and other elegant accomplishments of her period," Maxwell thought he might want to be an artist. On Saturdays he took lessons at the Chicago Art Institute. When I asked how he had become a writer instead, he mentioned a man named Pete Lemay who had been a member of the publicity department at Random House and "who said (when I asked him about Willa Cather, whom he knew and had just finished telling me about and it was all so unlikely that I said,

"Whatever made her a writer, do you suppose?")
'Why, what makes anybody a writer—deprivation
of course.' But apart from that the better question
would be would I have been a writer at all if my
friend Jack Scully had not come down with pleurisy
while he was working as a lifeguard. I went down
to Urbana with him to help him enroll—or rather
his parents said that he wasn't well enough to enroll in University and I offered to go with him and
so they agreed—if Jack hadn't got pleurisy I would
have enrolled as I planned to do in the Chicago Art
Institute and perhaps not have been a writer at all
but some kind of hack, for I wasn't all that talented.
I have a talent for copying, but no more."

After Harvard, Maxwell went back to Urbana
and taught freshman composition for two years.
He saw his life as a series of promotions within the
English department—assistant professor, professor,
professor emeritus and himself as eventually being
carried out in a box and decided that such a life
was not for him. By then it was 1933, "a bad time
to throw up one's job, but nevertheless I did it," he
wrote. "The money I had been saving to return to
Harvard for a PhD, I spent on a three months' trip
down through the West Indies, but I had in the
meantime, during the summer on the farm near
Portage, written my first novel, 'Bright Center of
Heaven' in a room at the top of what had been the
water tower. I used what went on under my nose,
and sometimes people made remarks at lunch that

I had already imagined them making during the morning's writing. The novel is lively and young, and full of sentences I obviously enjoyed writing and generalizations about life that aren't so. At the time what I wanted to know and the only thing I wanted to know about it was whether it was a novel. I took the manuscript to Zona Gale, who read it one night when she could not sleep, and at four o'clock came down to her study looking for the last chapter, which she assumed she must have left there and which did not exist. She said that it was a novel, to my relief. It took me twenty years to see that it had, in fact, ended a chapter too soon."

A long letter.

Written in 1999, the year before Maxwell died, describing how he was hired at *The New Yorker* and became an editor.

IN AUGUST 1936 I came to New York to get a job. My father gave me a hundred dollars and I had another hundred I didn't tell him about. I went to a friend of his, the president of an insurance company, to get the check cashed. He had always before been friendly and fatherly to me and this time he surprised me by being harsh and telling me I had no business trying to get a job in NYC, that I wouldn't make it here, and had better to go back to my long-haired friends in Wisconsin. About whom actually he knew nothing. It made me so furious that I talked myself into a job reading novels for Paramount Pictures. The first book they gave me was a long piece of trash called *Lady Cynthia Canden's Husband*. It was seven hundred pages long and they wanted my account to be five pages long, single or double spaced I don't remember, with five carbons. It took me two days to read the book and another to summarize the action and then I took it to be typed, since there was very little time left, which cost $5 and because it was a long book they gave me a special price of $7.50, leaving $2.50 in the clear for three days work. Then they gave me a second book, which I remember nothing about, and then I went for an interview with Katharine White.

Wolcott Gibbs had grown weary of part of his job, and they were looking for somebody to take his place in the art meeting and give the artists back their drawings with suggestions of what could be fixed, either picture or caption, or straight but tactful rejection. The fact that I had published a novel and a story in the *Atlantic* must have worked in my favor. At the end of the interview Mrs. White asked me how much I would want in the way of a salary. I had been told that I must ask for $35 a week, and she smiled and said, "I expect you could live on less." I could have lived nicely on $15. I couldn't make out whether the interview had been favorable or not. The thought of reading manuscripts for the movies didn't make me cheerful. I was living on the top floor of a brownstone rooming house on Lexington and 36th Street, or thereabouts. I remember the mattress was lumpy and there were bedbugs. I went down to the village and wandered around and decided to eat dinner at a Chinese restaurant on 8th Street, and though there were empty tables they made me sit with another person. In a bottomless depression I said to myself, There is no place for me anywhere in the world. And ate my dinner and came home and under my door was a telegram from Mrs. White that read, "Come to work on Monday at the price agreed upon."

They put me at a desk in the outer office near Mrs. White's door. On Monday I had nothing whatever to do but sit and look at a self-portrait by Thurber drawn on the wall. The place was full of his drawings on the walls. On Tuesday the artists (as they were called, actually they were cartoonists) brought their work in and Tuesday afternoon the art meeting took place, in a room large enough to hold a big table and four chairs. The drawings and covers were propped up so that they could be seen, and everybody had knitting needles, of plastic, so they could point to details of the drawings. I had one but didn't use it. Ross was in charge. By common agreement "rough," that is, drawings that indicated what the picture would be like but were only sketches, were rejected or approved—if approved the artist would then make a finished drawing and submit it the following week. Most of the ideas were so forced that I found the meeting deadly. Also, I suffered from insomnia and was afraid if I didn't sleep the night before the art meeting I wouldn't know whether something was funny or not.

On Wednesday Rae Irwin went over the spots and I sat beside him. If I liked a drawing, he good-naturedly put it in the yes pile. On Thursday the artists came in to get their work back and I talked to them all day long. What was so odd was that they all put themselves in their pictures. Soglow *was* the little King. Alajalov was elegant, Arthur Dove wore yellow gloves, Perry Barlow was kind and natural. Arno and Miss Hokinson were too important for me to deal with, and were dealt with by Katharine White or Gibbs. Mrs. White suggested I read the scrapbooks of back issues, so then I had something to do besides sit and look at the walls. One day Mrs. White brought me a pile of manuscripts to write rejection letters for, which I did, and after she had read my letter she said, "Mr. Maxwell, did you ever teach school?" It was a fact I had withheld during my interview, thinking it wouldn't be a mark in my favor. When I told her I had she said, "It is not the work of the editor to tell the writer how to write." End of discussion. Actually it is, but it must be done in such a way that the writer doesn't know you are doing it.

One day Gibbs brought me a story by Kay Boyle that had been accepted and asked me if I'd like to try editing it. He didn't explain what editing was. I saw that it was overwritten and treated it as I would've treated a rough version of a story I was writing. That is to say, I cleaned it up and to my surprise he sent it to be printed. The next story he gave me was a piece of back of the book humor and I fell on my face. It was largely much ado about nothing, and my editing, Gibbs said revealed this, but wasn't the way to go about editing back of the book humor. Then Mrs. White took me in hand and taught me how to edit manuscripts.

Then they tried me on preparing author's proofs for Gibbs, to save him time. He had the fastest mind I have ever encountered and I tried very hard to finish the question before he had answered it but never succeeded. He was always patient with me and only flared up once over some detail about a kind of cocktail, and I said I didn't know anything about such drinks and he took it only for a second as a criticism of him until he realized it was only the simple truth.

When I had been there a few months I was given a new job after which time no longer hung heavy on my hands. The proofreaders' queries and Ross's were combined on a master proof which Mrs. White or Gibbs sent to the author. If followed, the proofreaders' suggestions would make the writing more correct but lifeless. Ross's queries on manuscripts were always to the point but he had so many galleys to read—the whole magazine in fact—and he read the galleys too hurriedly, which resulted in misimpressions. His galleys usually had, even for a slight back of the book story, about sixty queries, of which four or five were acute and taken seriously. The rest were an effort on his part to correct the facts of the story so that they would be consistent with something the author hadn't said. It was my job to spare Gibbs and Mrs. White having to consider them. The galleys were an education in editing.

Anyway when I dealt with galley proofs they gave me an office at last. Somewhere along the first three months I felt I wasn't going to be fired and sent my father his hundred dollars and when he got it my stepmother said that he wept. It had been the great fear of his life that I would be financially irresponsible and sponge off other people.

Gibbs withdrew more and more from his editing job into profile writing and also from the art meeting and in so far as I was able I took his place. With delightfully increasing salary. Every time I was promoted I would go to him and ask how much I should ask for and he always told me the right answer. Somewhere along about my second year I had a telephone call from my editor at *Harper's* saying that "They Came Like Swallows" had been chosen as a dual selection of the Book of the Month Club and the initial payment was $8000. It was so much money I had to lean against the wall for support. Then I went and told Gibbs. And then I invited the Whites to dinner and the theater. I asked Gibbs where to take them and he told me. It was small and the most elegant restaurant by far that I had ever been in. I took what was the most imaginable amount of cash to pay for it—$35 and that's exactly what it came to.

Then Andy White began to be restless and want to live in Maine, which meant that Katharine had to leave a job she had created and was very happy in. *The New Yorker* hired a friend of Andy's, Gus Lobrano, who was working on *Town and Country*, and I took him into my office to break him in and we became friends. I assumed I would replace Mrs. White as fiction editor, which was pure foolishness on my part because the job was just as much a matter of dealing with humorists, perhaps more so, than fiction writers. When my uncle died in Illinois and I went to the funeral, I came back to find that Lobrano had been moved into KSW's office, which meant that he was slated to become her successor. I thought the hell with them, I will become a writer if that's the way things are. So I asked for an appointment with Ross to tell him I was resigning and he invited me (for the first time) to lunch at the Algonquin. I see I have left out something important. After a couple of years I was taken out of the fiction department and worked directly under Ross, the job being known as the A issue editor. I loved working with him. He was very funny and not the kook he is often made out to be. I had been told that once in a fit of temper he threw a telephone at Mrs. White. He never even raised his voice at me. Once I told him something that I thought was correct, only to find, when I left his office, that I should have given him the exact contrary advice. I remember leaning against the door and thinking I can't go in there and tell him I told him the wrong answer. Then my upbringing asserted itself and I went in and told him I had given him the wrong information and he didn't turn a hair. He wasn't interested in my mistake, only in the right answer. Anyway, we sat down to a table in the Algonquin and I told him I wanted to leave, and he said, "I was going to offer you the job of second in command of the magazine." Which rocked me a little, but he didn't urge me to reconsider and if I had it wouldn't matter. Very soon I wouldn't have been working for the magazine at all, because the second in command always got blamed for whatever went wrong and sooner or later was fired.

The five days a week job was so consuming that I had no other life. I lived in the Village, in Patchen Place, in a very small two room apartment and didn't have a telephone until Mrs. White's secretary insisted on it, and when it did ring I didn't answer it. I was with people all day long and couldn't stand anymore.

I went to Santa Fe with Morris Burge and we had a house there for the summer and every night had dinner with his fiancé and we drove through the country around Santa Fe. Morris knew everybody but I asked him not to introduce me to people and gradually in the course of the summer let down . . . .

From the New Mexico journal, 1940.

To DO A book about a journey, using the literal excitement as a point of departure for a reflective novel, the symbolism for pattern, and as a final point in the fact that each day—from waking to unconscious, undreaming sleep is as much a journey, as subject to delay, accident, misdirection, as the trip from New York to Santa Fe. Or that from birth to death is only a long journey made up of daily stages from Asheville to Knoxville, from Knoxville to Memphis, from morning to night.

The nervous frustration of people who are ready to go and cannot, either because they are not free, or because they have arbitrarily set a day of departure and cannot go until that day arrives. Or because they want to stay in one place, actually, and cannot quite cover up the fact that on a turning earth in a mechanically revolving universe there is no one place to stand still on.

The ways of approaching a journey. The man who at the beginning of a journey sees himself coming back, putting his suitcases in the back of the car, riding home from the airport from which he is about to depart, covering his ears with his hands so that he will not hear the two blasts of the boat's whistle as it signals for the pilot to come on board.

Or the man—the saddest of all voyageurs—who leaves each place in turn without reluctance, with no desire to return.

Or the woman who prefers movement—change—continuous journeying because new faces, new places and climate do not mirror honestly, and it is possible therefore to keep one step ahead of Time, though moving always in the knowledge of accidental death. Or those centrifugal people whose fingers cannot hold them to a place even when they try not to let go. Or the homesick ones who by a too constant movement lose one by one all of their possessions—their native accent, the certainty of a local point of view, the ability to identify themselves with a particular kind of sky, or the sounds, say of windmills creaking, or the way the land is, in certain remembered places, so that in New Mexico their talk reflects Bermuda, and in Bermuda it is again and again of Barbados, but never of Wisconsin or Illinois or Ohio or wherever they were originally; never of home.

Or those people who travel with everything—books, clothes, for all four seasons, shoe trees, medicines, binoculars, and telephone numbers. They are the unwilling travelers. The willing ones travel light—by freight or by jerking their thumb, with 10 days' destination beyond the next town of more than five thousand inhabitants. And no immediate object beyond food and a comfortable place to sleep. No ultimate object beyond a free death. They make appointments to meet people at such and such a day on the steps of the courthouse of Amarillo, Texas, but they do not keep these appointments because they cannot. They go too long without food, the heat gets them, they eat nothing but ripe tomatoes for days until they are no longer sure of what they are doing and have to be helped. But when they get well again and are able to set up a short while each day, they begin to think about where they will go next and they make new appointments.

Or the knowledge that one gets of other people only on a journey—their good temper, their strength—whether or not they had access to the reservoirs of strength accumulated by their ancestors. The hammering of personal characteristics which, on a slight acquaintance, are charming and on a closer acquaintance are deadly, possible only on a protracted journey. After which they may seem, as Huxley has them, something to rule out of one's life—as R. F. does, I suspect, as part of the general evil, not intrinsically different from theft or murder. Or perhaps, through sufficient detachment, and seen by the light of love, they are not evil after all, but merely heart-breaking.

But how to be always on a journey and see what one sees only when one is standing still. A black cat in the garden, moving through iris blades, behind a lilac bush, on a garden wall—how to keep oneself sufficiently quiet so that when the cat, in one spring, reaches the top of the garden wall, turns down again and disappears, one will see it and remember it, and not be absorbed at the moment in the dryness of one's hands.

If one missed the cat jumping over the garden wall it might not matter, unless to give up seeing clearly, to be uncertain in smells, to be unable to distinguish, by touch, one body from another is to reach too soon the end of the Whole Journey, to die in childhood. But the cat is everything and one must stop worrying about the dryness, the difficulty because of the altitude, of getting a complete breath, the cold wind that blows through the apple blossoms, the dust, the colors of one's shoes.

In traveling it is not enough to see the fishermen drawing in their nets, the villages lying against the shelf of palm trees, smells, or the double rainbow over Fort-de-France. One must somehow contrive, if only for a week, only over night, to live in the houses of people, so that one knows first the elementary things—which doors bang, how the telephone sounds, where they dry dishtowels, and how their lungs feel when they wake in the night and reach blindly toward the foot of the bed for the extra covers. And through all their things, their books, their china, their pictures—the picture that is hung too high, and especially the paintings which are not good, the one they have been compelled to paint themselves, which are not good but seem better if one stays a week and knows the countryside in more than one kind of light; through these things, through the rugs on the floor, the carving on the beds, the sharpness and the shape of their scissors, one must find the people who used to live there but who now are in New York, or now are dead.

From *The Folded Leaf* **(1945).**

ON THE TENTH of March, which was the anniversary of Mrs. Peters' death, Mr. Peters and Lymie got up early and went down to the Union Station. From Chicago to the small town they had once lived in was a trip of a little less than two hours, on the Chicago, Burlington, and Quincy Railroad. They made this journey every year. The scenery was not interesting—the cornfields of Illinois in March are dreary and monotonous—and there was no pleasure attached to the trip in the mind of either of them. But to live in the world at all is to be committed to some kind of a journey.

If you are ready to go and cannot, either because you are not free or because you have no one to travel with—or if you have arbitrarily set a date for your departure and dare not go until that day arrives, you still have no cause for concern. Without knowing it, you have actually started. On a turning earth, in a mechanically revolving universe, there is no place to stand still.

Accidents, misdirections, overexcitement, heat, crowds and heartbreaking delays you must expect when you go on a journey, just as you expect to have dreams at night. Whether or not you enjoy yourself at all depends on your state of mind. The man who travels with everything he owns, books, clothes for every season, shoe trees, a dinner jacket, medicines, binoculars, magazines and telephone numbers—the unwilling traveler—and the man who leaves each place in turn without reluctance, with no desire ever to come back, obviously cannot be making the same journey, even though their tickets are identical. The same thing holds good for the woman who was once beautiful and who now has to resort to movement, change, continuous packing and unpacking, in order to avoid the reality that awaits her in the smallest mirror. And for the ambitious young man who by a too constant shifting around has lost all of his possessions, including his native accent and the ability to identify himself with a particular kind of sky or the sound, let us say, of windmills creaking; so that in New Mexico his talk reflects Bermuda, and in Bermuda it is again and again of Barbados that he is reminded, but never of Iowa or Wisconsin or Indiana, never of home.

Though people usually have long complicated tickets which they expect the conductor to take from them in due time, the fact is that you don't need to bother with a ticket at all. If you were willing to travel lightly, you can also dispense with the train. Cars and trucks are continually stopping at filling stations and at corners where there is an overhead stoplight. By jerking your thumb you will almost certainly get a ride to the next town of more than two thousand inhabitants where (chances are) you will manage to get something to eat and a place to sleep for a night or so, even if it's only the county jail.

The appointment you have made to meet somebody at such and such a day at noon on the steps of the courthouse at Amarillo, Texas, you may have to forget. Especially if you go too long without food or with nothing but stolen ripe tomatoes, so that suddenly you are not sure of what you are saying. Or if the heat gets you, and when you wake up you are in a hospital ward. But after you start to get well again and are able to set up a short while each day, there will be time to begin thinking about where you will go next. And if you like, you can always make new appointments.

The great, the universal problem is how to be always on a journey and yet see what you would see if it were only possible for you to stay home: a black cat in a garden, moving through iris blades behind a lilac bush. How to keep sufficiently detached and quiet inside so that when the cat in one spring reaches the top of the garden wall, turns down again, and disappears, you will see and remember it, and not be absorbed at that moment in the dryness of your hands.

If you missed that particular cat jumping over one out of so many garden walls, it ought not to matter, but it does apparently. The cat seems to be everything. Seeing clearly is everything. Being certain as to smells, being able to remember sounds and to distinguish by touch one object, one body from another. And it is not enough to see the fishermen drawing in their wide circular net, the tropical villages lying against a shelf of palm trees, or the double rainbow over Fort-de-France. You must somehow contrive, if only for a week or only overnight, to live in the houses of people, so that at least you know the elementary things—which doors sometimes bang when a sudden wind springs up; where the telephone book is kept; and how their lungs feel when they waken in the night and reach blindly toward the foot of the bed for the extra cover.

You are in duty bound to go through all of their possessions, to feel their curtains and look for the trade name on the bottom of their best dinner plates and stand before their pictures (especially the one they have been compelled to paint themselves, which is not a good painting but seems better if you stay long enough to know the country in more than one kind of light) and lift the lids of their cigarette boxes and sniff their pipe tobacco and open, one by one, their closet doors. You should test the sharpness and shape of their scissors. You may play their radio and try, with your fingernail, to open the locked door of the liquor cabinet. You may even read any letters that they have been so careless as to leave around. Through all of these things, through the attic and the cellar and the toolshed you must go searching until you find the people who live here or who used to live here but now are in London or Acapulco or Galesburg, Illinois. Or who now are dead.

In New Mexico.

THE DEAD MAY be inaccessible but sometimes they aren't. The dead man who built this house still lives in it. His wife has not married again, but if she does, I don't know what will happen to her, unless she moves. She will have to do that. There is no room, either on the bookshelves, or in the closets, some of which are locked, for another man's things. He was a writer, he wrote three books, one of them about flagellants, and people speak of him with affection, and are unresigned to his dying when he did. His picture is in this room. His forehead was high, his lips were more sensitive than his eyes, I think—though you cannot always tell with photographs. You cannot even be sure that his eyes were habitually focused on the mountains which lie all in a circle around Santa Fe. But the books which he left behind support the mouth mainly. Though some of them support the eyes. And what I would like to know is whether the eyes were winning, during that last illness, or whether the last part of him left alive was his mouth. Because there are all of those books, so badly illustrated, so imprecisely written. *Justine*, *Eastern Shame Girl*, the oriental ones, the privately printed ones with photographs and drawings of bodies in unhappy unsatisfied positions. And through them I know his unhappiness, the imagination that must, at times, have heated the body even past exhaustion, past will, past his last illness perhaps. Pareto [an Italian economist of the nineteenth century] is in the little house where he worked, but not Plato and Plato would've been of actual help.

Almost no sleep last night, though I didn't mind. I lay on one side and then the other and eventually, as I thought I might, dreamt of home. Too much coffee after dinner, but I dreamed of home because I found, that evening, another one, another place that will be as familiar to me sometimes as all the other places I have lived in happily. The Rio Grande flows through the front yard but it is smaller than the creek where we used to go fishing, when I was a child. The geography books didn't say it would be like that, hemmed in by mesas, and likely before the summer comes to be even smaller. And the woman who was supposed to be strange and distant, served us a beautiful lamb ragout, and was kindness itself. And after dinner when we came outside, Orion's belt hung just over the hills, and I put the whole place away for safe keeping.

Yesterday morning the Spanish American gardener cleaned out the winter's dust and rotting leaves from the fish pond, and while Morris and I sat on our haunches, watching him catch the big goldfish and the five little ones that had no color, in a white granite pan, I thought what a good beginning page for a book. I still think in beginnings, like a man forever putting on his hat, but the sun and the new bicycle—rather than new secondhand bicycle, the morning glories that bloom, that ought to bloom along the fence a month from now, by their continuous nature may change it. To think of the end instead of the beginning has been for a long time—I don't know how long, twenty years perhaps—to think of death. And because I don't want to think of it, or write of it, not through fear but now, I think, merely from choice, my direction is toward the beginning of things. But it is an obvious kind of nearsightedness, and there must, obviously, be exercises to correct it. When I raised my eyes a minute ago I saw a windmill a hundred yards away, and it was revolving steadily in the sunlight, without any beginning and probably, for years to come, without any end. The air is never quite still here, and the windmill may slow up—is now—but I don't think it will stop. But how to do that? How to write a book that will go round and round, faster or slower, without a beginning or an end, but only night and day and night and day. The windmill is absolutely still. Now it is going quite fast again, proving that an end which is followed immediately by a beginning is neither end nor beginning but a continuity of a different kind, a rhythm that is more accurate, as an analogy, to living, than continuous revolving, which can only have a single meaning.

Realized yesterday, watching through binoculars a gardener mowing grass that the reality we accept through the senses is almost never perceived through one sense alone. A man mowing grass should be accompanied by the sound of a lawnmower, to be believed. Because the air is thin and clear, and because of the binoculars one can separate the sense of sight and the sense of hearing from their usual union. And then merely by closing one's eyes the man mowing the lawn becomes an idea only, and one has to look to the mind for confirmation of his actuality, not to the senses. Which may account for the inward look on the faces of the blind, and the strained expression of the deaf. With the failure of sight and hearing to confirm one another, both the deaf and blind must depend upon general knowledge, must go constantly to the mind for evidence, rather than for the meaning of the evidence they have received through sensory perception. And the boundary between the natural and the supernatural (which is mostly suspected by the fact that the senses don't jibe) must be far less, go to a different degree, the blind falling back upon the sense of touch, the deaf making the eyes do the work of both seeing and hearing. To both a great many things cannot exist. The windmill from here makes no sound, and if I were blind would not be there. The deaf, on the other hand, are always several seconds slow, and that, in all probability accounts for the strain. They are forever recovering from impressions which have come upon them too suddenly, with no warning sound. They must be ready. The blind are more serene, because they had decided upon the sensory evidence submitted by the sense of touch, or smell, or hearing, they are involved in no action.

And one way or another, for large sections of all time, we are either blind or deaf, sometimes both. A man passed the house this morning, and I saw him out of the bathroom window; saw him returning with a little girl in blue overalls. And even so I failed to perceive that his wife died this morning. A blind person might've heard it in his step, a deaf person in the way he turned his face to the sun. But all I saw was a man getting older and heavier before it was time for him to get old and heavy.

The Folded Leaf.

IN DESERT COUNTRY the air is never still. You raise your eyes and see a windmill a hundred yards away, revolving in the sunlight, without any apparent beginning and for years to come without any end. It may seem to slow up and stop but that is only because it is getting ready to go round and round again, faster and faster, night and day, week in, week out. The end that is followed immediately by a beginning is neither end nor beginning. Whatever is alive must be continuous. There is no life that doesn't go on and on, even the life that is in water and in stones. Listen and you hear children's voices, a dog's soft padded steps, a man hammering, a man sharpening a scythe. Each of them is repeated, the same sound, starting and stopping like a windmill. From where you are, the windmill makes no sound, and if you were blind would not be there. A man mowing grass must be accompanied by the sound of a lawn mower to be believed. If you have discovered him with the aid of binoculars then you have also discovered that reality is almost never perceived through one of the senses alone. Withdraw the binoculars and where is the man mowing grass? You have to look to the mind for confirmation of his actuality, which may account for the inward look on the faces of the blind, the strained faces of the deaf who are forever recovering from impressions which have come upon them too suddenly with no warning sound.

But who is not, in one way or another, for large sections of time, blind or deaf or both? Mr. Peters passed the Forbes's house on his way to the hospital and Mrs. Forbes saw him, without knowing who he was, when she glanced out of her living room windows. She saw him returning an hour later and, even so, failed to perceive that for the first time in many years he had tried to speak from his heart and had failed. A person really blind might have heard it in his step, a deaf person would have seen it in the way he turned his face to the sun. All that Mrs. Forbes saw was a man getting old and heavy before his time.

New Mexico.

THE AIR IS nervous this morning. Wind in the poplars, a train, a school bell, a fly. All sounds building toward something which may not be good. A car horn, a spade striking hard ground, a dog barking, a child's voice blocks away, a bird in the Chinese elms. Two sparrows, and restless clouds all over the sky. The only quiet anywhere is in the gardener, Tranqulino, squatting on his haunches, in the apple orchard above the house. Day after day he tends a garden for a woman who is always coming but never arrives. His iris blooms, his roses fade, his potted geraniums stare out of the windows of the shut up house. From time to time he empties the goldfish pool and puts clean water in it. I think he no longer believes in her coming or in what he does. I think he knows that there is nothing to draw her here now but ashes strewn some years ago on a mountaintop, and that is not enough. Or perhaps things hold her in the east. Obligations and responsibilities. Or else she is waiting for a sign.

The sound of somebody chopping wood drew me out of the front gate and into the empty lot across the road where I found blue lupines growing, and saw Indian blankets airing on a clothesline, and a man adding a room onto an adobe house, and another rolling a tennis court, and two others worrying over a truck, and another delivering the morning mail. I also saw a man cutting wood and looked up to see a storm coming over the mountain, brought on by the uneasy wind in the poplars.

The Folded Leaf.

THERE ARE THINGS in the desert which aren't to be found anywhere else. You can see a hundred miles in every direction, when you step out of your front door, and at night the stars are even brighter than they are at sea. If you cannot find indoors what you should find, then go to the window and look at the mountains, revealed after two days of uncertainty, of no future beyond the foot-hills which lie in a circle around the town. If it is not actually cold, if you aren't obliged to hug the fire, then go outside, by all means, even though the air is nervous, and you hear wind in the poplars, a train, a school bell, a fly—all sounds building toward something which may not be good. For reassurance there is also a car horn, a spade striking hard ground, a dog barking, and an un-identifiable bird in the Chinese elm. For further comfort there is the gardener, an old Spaniard, squatting on his haunches near the house next door. He is cleaning out the winter's rubbish and rotting leaves from the fishpond. While you sit on your haunches watching him, he will catch, in a white enamel pan, the big goldfish and the five little ones that have as yet no color. Day after day he tends this garden for a woman who is always coming back but who never arrives. Patience is to be learned from him. His iris blooms, his roses fade, his potted pink geraniums stare out of the windows of the shut-up house. It is possible that he no longer believes in the woman's coming, but nevertheless, from time to time, he empties the goldfish pool and puts fresh water in it.

If the sound of somebody chopping wood draws you out of the front gate and into the empty lot across the road, you will find blue lupines growing and see blankets airing on a clothesline, and you can talk to the man who is adding a room onto his adobe house. A great deal is to be learned from him. Also from the man chopping wood, who knows even now that there is a thunderstorm coming over the mountains, brought on by the uneasy wind in the poplars.

New Mexico.

HALF OF WHAT there is to know about Anglos is implied in the fact that there is no word for addressing a stranger and conveying instantaneous approval and liking; no word to indicate a general warmth of heart. For the most part Anglos don't like the people they already know, let alone strangers. They sleep alone if they can, they have lost all memory of a common table, they go to tremendous expense to keep their bones from mingling with the dust of their mothers and fathers, whom they didn't always like either. Given a free choice most Anglos would choose an incubator.

For that reason rather than any real delight in pink houses and oversized flowers, they are impelled to visit hot countries. An open fire can only thaw out so much.

Spanish Americans do have a word "primo"—*cousin*—which conveys everything—their liking, their willingness to share the clothes on their back, the food on their table, their fire, as long as there is any need. The same warmth of heart is extended occasionally to animals.

The ceiling is lifted and there is after two days an uncertain sunlight. It is not actually cold outside but for the lack of confidence I hug the fire. My head is heavy and I cannot work. The little boys of *en medio* have turned into blue denim statues, caught as they were about to run away. And how to give them back their freedom and their fright is the question. I see them there, but in a frame, not breathing.

One of them has patches in the seat of his pants, his overalls which must have come to him from many others, with some—a very little perhaps—of their animal warmth still left—so that when he is alone or sent on an errand, for water maybe, his brothers are with him. And all through the day until night comes, when they are with him actually, crosswise in the bed, and curled around him like puppies.

Another had a gray cotton jacket with cartoons on the back, and the mark of the world's cheapness was on him, innocent though he was of any world beyond the valley. And there was another who was not innocent but born knowing the worst, though not where to find it. And the other two have Indians for ancestors and would—perhaps even now were doing things in a way that was different from the others, for reasons hidden but still urgent. Even their sleep is, in all probability, different, being full of dancing and dreams which turned out to be prophecies.

The Folded Leaf.

IF YOU GO and live for a while in desert country it is possible that you may encounter some Spanish boys, barefoot, wearing blue denim overalls. It is important that you who have moral standards but no word for addressing a stranger and conveying instantaneous approval and liking, no word to indicate a general warmth of heart; who sleep alone if you can and have lost all memory of a common table and go to tremendous lengths to keep your bones from mingling with the bones of other people—it is vitally important that you meet the little Spanish boys.

If you speak to them too abruptly they may run away, or they may even turn into statues; and how to give them back their freedom and release them from their fright is something that you alone can solve. One of them will have patches on the seat of his overalls, which have come down to him from many older brothers with some of their animal magic still left. When he is sent for water, his brothers are there to protect him. All through the day he wears their magic, until night, when his brothers are with him actually, crosswise in the bed, or curled against him on a hard pallet on the floor.

One of the little Spanish boys will use expressions which were current in the time of Cervantes. Another will have a gray cotton sweatshirt with Pop-Eye the Sailor on the back—the mark of the world and its cheapness upon him, innocent though he is of any world beyond this desert valley. And there will be another who is not innocent but born knowing the worst, though perhaps not where to find it. And two others will have Indians for ancestors and, for reasons that are hidden from them but urgent, will do things in a way that is different from the way that the others, the pure Spanish, the Mexicans, chose. Even the sleep of the little boys with Indian blood is different being (in all probability) full of dancing and dreams which turn out to be prophecies.

The little Spanish boys have a word—*primo*, meaning cousin—which they use to convey their liking for strangers, their willingness to share the clothes on their back, the food on their table, their fire if they have one. This same uncritical love is offered frequently to goats, burros, dogs, and chickens, and it will be extended to you.

From *The Outermost Dream* (1989).

Note from the beginning of *The Outermost Dream*, Maxwell's book of essays and reviews.

IN THE SUMMER of 1948, chance deposited my wife and me in the bleachers of a tiny one-ring circus playing under a tent on the outskirts of Florence. As the afternoon wore on, the equestrienne's little girl performed on the tight-wire for the first time, while her mother and the roustabouts looked on anxiously. The roustabouts shed their grey coveralls in order to juggle hoops and ninepins or hang head-down from the flying trapeze. The lions had diarrhea. Because it was so clearly a family affair and the performers made up for the absence of numbers by the variety of their talents, it reminded me of the *New Yorker* office, and where from the beginning people did more than the thing they were hired to do. John Mosher read unsolicited manuscripts and covered the movies. Philip Hamburger wrote Profiles and for a season was the music critic. Several cartoonists owe their immortality to the fact that E. B. White had recaptioned a drawing that was about to be returned to them. And there wasn't anything that Wolcott Gibbs couldn't or didn't do. Edith Oliver doubled as critic for off-Broadway theater and as book editor, and from time to time would say to me, "I have a book that I think might interest you." Looking the gift horse in the mouth (lead reviews were well-paid) I would say, "Can I see it?"—for I led a double life too. Three days a week I was a fiction editor and the other four days I was a novelist and worked at home. I enjoyed reading manuscripts because there was always the possibility that a first-rate story would turn up in the morning mail, but I felt no inclination to read, let alone write about, a book that didn't appeal to me. Her instinct for what I couldn't say no to was all but infallible.

Reading is rapture (or if it isn't, I put the book down meaning to go on with it later, and escape out the side door). A felicitously turned sentence can induce it. Or a description. Or unexpected behavior. Or ordinary behavior raised to the nth degree. Or intolerable suspense, as with the second half of Conrad's *Victory*. Or the forward movement of prose that is bent only on saying what the writer has to say. Or dialogue that carries with it the unconscious flowering of character. Or, sometimes, a fact.

I was never asked to deal with a work of fiction and if I had been I would've said no. Too much of a busman's holiday. Also, after you have said whether it does or does not have the breath of life, what standards are you going to invoke when confronted with a thing that, like a caterpillar, consumes whatever is at hand? A long narrative requires impersonation, hallucinating when you don't know the answer, turning water into wine, making a silk purse out of a string of colored scarves and extracting a white rabbit from a sow's ear, knowing how and when to hold the carrot in front of the donkey's nose, and sublime confidence. "The house was full of that poetic atmosphere of dullness and silence which always accompanies the presence of an engaged couple." That sort of thing will keep any reader from escaping out the side door. But diaries, memoirs, published correspondence, biography and autobiography—which is what I was asked to consider—do not spring from prestidigitation or require a long apprenticeship. They tell what happened—what people said and did and wore and ate and hoped for and were afraid of, and in detail after often unimaginable detail they refresh our idea of existence and hold oblivion at arm's length. Looked at broadly, what happened always has meaning, pattern, form, and authenticity. One can classify, analyze, arrange in the order of importance, and judge any or all of these things, or one can simply stand back and view the whole with wonder.

Village Poets (1937).

Maxwell occasionally wrote stories for *The New Yorker*'s Talk of the Town department, which in those days were unsigned. Here are three.

YOU MAY HAVE noticed that the Raven Poetry Circle was holding its fifth annual outdoor poetry show last week on the south side of Washington Square, by the tennis courts. It's a good deal like the outdoor art show, but smaller, and attracts less attention. The poets come down from their garrets along about one o'clock (at which time the Village is regarded as officially awake), pin their poems up on the wall, and then sit around hopefully on soapboxes until sundown. Sometimes the poems are typed, sometimes they are written out in longhand on bright-colored cardboard. Prices range from ten cents to a couple of dollars, with the average somewhere around a quarter. We were there at five in the afternoon and business was slow. Passersby would stop and read the first three or four lines of a sonnet, as far as "daffodil" or "ecstasy," and then, as a rule, go on down the sidewalk. We found two examples of light verse and a rather stirring attack on militarism which began

One-two-three-four
War War War

but in general the trend of the show was away from reality and toward the Ivory Tower. No mention of Sullivan Street or the Sixth Avenue "L," or, indeed, of anything less poetic than love, or the moon, or winter weather.

The gentleman in charge of the show, Mr. Francis Lambert McCrudden, had gone across the street into the park to eat an ice-cream cone. We followed him there and found him a pleasant elderly man, quite willing to talk about poetry or himself. He once had a trucking business, but is now retired, he told us. He's a great admirer of the works of Edgar Allan Poe, and keeps a stuffed raven in his room, just above the chamber door. We asked him how the poetry show came about and he said he reasons that if the artists were going to bring their paintings out on the sidewalk year after year, the poets might as well do the same thing. Offhand we couldn't give him any reason they shouldn't.

It is up to Mr. McCrudden, as founder of the Poetry Circle, to assign sections along the tennis-court wall. Once in a while there is some jockeying for position, but usually he doesn't have much trouble. The place of honor went this year to Maxwell Bodenheim, who is the only one of the Village poets we seemed to have heard of before. He was smoking a corncob pipe, and had on a baggy gray suit, dark-blue shirt, and red tie. What we noticed about him particularly, though, was a way he had of talking to people directly and intensely with his eyes shut. Four of his poems were offered for sale at two dollars apiece, with the added inducement that they had been autographed by the author on his birthday. Bodenheim is not a member of the Raven Poetry Circle, but he was glad to lend his presence and his poems to the occasion. The Poetry Circle meets once a month and has between twenty and thirty members. It used to have more, but in recent years there has been a falling off, a number of the best poets having gone on WPA and two or three having drunk themselves to death.

Knapsack King (1957).
with Brendan Gill

"THE KNAPSACK KING of France is at the Barbizon-Plaza," a Royalist friend of ours told us the other day, so off to the Barbizon-Plaza we went, and there, presiding over a booth at the French Exhibition of Sporting Goods in the Barbizon Room, we found him: M. Gabriel Lafuma, of Lafuma Freres in Anneyron—forty miles south of Lyon in the Rhone Valley. He was surrounded by knapsacks called Lafuma Junior, Lafuma Senior, Lafuma Guide, Lafuma Camping, Lafuma Super-Senior, Lafuma Super-Guide, and Lafuma Super-Camping. "Are you the knapsack king of France?" we asked. He hesitated, and said that there are three knapsack kings of France, all wholesale. Victor Lafuma is the senior knapsack king, Alfred Lafuma is the No. 2 knapsack king, and Gabriel is the baby knapsack king. All are brothers, and all are partners in the *maison* Lafuma Freres, manufacturers of—and we quote from a court document, which Gabriel handed us—"*sacs pour la montagne et le camping, sacs pour tous les sports d'equipes, tables et sieges pour le pique-nique et le camping.*" Victor is in charge of production, Alfred is the treasurer, and Gabriel is responsible for sales, purchases, and design. "We are placing our knapsacks in this country for the first time," M. Lafuma said. "Tensing, the Sherpa guide who reached the top of Mt. Everest with the Hilary expedition last spring, used Lafuma knapsacks. Our house was founded in 1924, and in 1936 we developed the knapsack with *armature*—a flexible steel frame that fits the back of the wearer. This holds the bag up, making it more comfortable to carry, and permits air to pass between it and its wearer's back, reducing sweat. I used to do some mountain climbing myself and realized something was missing in my knapsack. It was *armature!* We now furnish the French army with all its knapsack *armatures*—six hundred thousand frames last year. We also sell them around fifty thousand knapsacks a year, to go with the frames; the rest of the knapsacks they buy from other manufacturers, but they follow our designs. And last year we filled a special order for sixty thousand knapsacks, with frames, for the troops in Indo-China—the French troops that is. We hope to interest the American Army."

M. Lafuma, who has a mustache and a jaunty expression, was born in 1904 in Anneyron, where his father was superintendent of a tannery. The youngest Lafuma studied leatherwork and automobile-body manufacture in his early teens, and worked in a car-body factory in Lyon for a while before becoming the No. 3 King. "I passed an examination to be a master saddler in the army but decided to join my brothers in business instead," he said. "We have a factory with two hundred and fifty workmen and a daily production of four thousand knapsacks, including small ones, without *armatures*, for tourists. We have a patent on the *armature*. In 1940, we turned out forty-five thousand Army knapsacks in twenty-five days, for the Narvik expedition. My brothers and I each have a son in the business. I like to play bridge and tennis, and shoot pheasants and rabbits. I've shot very few rabbits recently, as the rabbits in my neighborhood all got rabbit disease and died before I could shoot them. In France, we outfit the Boy Scouts and Girl Scouts. This is my first visit to America. New York has made a formidable impression on me. I am in ecstasies before Rockefeller Center."

We urged M. Lafuma to come again, and backed out of his presence.

Artifacts (1949).
with Brendan Gill and John Brooks

HAVING HEARD A lot about the depleted state of the Reservoir and a little about the ancient roads and ruins and boundary walls that have been slowly coming into sight as the water level has been dropping, we drove up there and had a thorough archaeological look around. The reservoir seems indeed frighteningly low—its shoreline, rocky and fringed with trees, is nearly forty feet above the present surface of the water, and boats lie tethered high on its dry flanks, at a rakish angle better suited to toboggans than to boats. One can walk dry-shod over what has for nearly fifty years been dark and weedy lake bottom, and residents of the vicinity, exploring this exposed Atlantis, have begun to set themselves up as authorities on the lost American civilization of 1900. It was then that the so-called new Croton Reservoir[1] was built, greatly increasing the capacity of the original Croton Reservoir, which had been built in 1842.

Our observations began at Old Dam Bridge, just east of the point at which the Taconic State Parkway crosses the reservoir. There a flat, caked, treeless area obviously intended to be under water and showing a skeleton of criss-crossed stone field walls, with gaunt rows of stumps and here and there the low, moldering foundation of some old building—in normal times, we thought a fine hideout for pickle or bass. Proceeding to the gatehouse of the reservoir, we introduced ourself to Mr. John Tompkins, and he accompanied us on a long stroll along the wide and widening shore. As we walked, we discovered several interesting artifacts—a tin can, which dissolved into rusty powder when we kicked it; a bottle, which, though it lacked a label, had the look of once having held whiskey (it had held water too long to smell of anything); and a few clamshells, which we found inexplicable, as did Tompkins. He pointed toward some substantial brick-and-stone ruins. "That's the caretaker's house of the old reservoir," he said. "Those two walls running along there like arms, they held

---

1 Maxwell's house in the country is about a mile from the Croton Reservoir.

the road between them. That foundation just across the road was the Palmer Hotel. They used to have Democratic conventions there in the old days." Mr. Tompkins told us that an ancient stone bridge across the Croton River lies out of sight in what was the original Croton Reservoir, which constitutes the lowest part of the present reservoir.

A couple of miles farther on, Mr. Tompkins led us onto a bridge, which he said was the new Pines Bridge, over which Washington and his troops once marched. Mr. Tompkins identified the foundations of the Village schoolhouse, a race track, and the site of a cemetery that had been moved—"bodily," Tompkins said—to the town of Amawalk. As we stood on the bridge a lady came up and joined us. "I used to walk across this bridge on my way to Sunday school," she said. "That was forty years ago. I can remember when the water was so high that the spray blinded you when the wind blew."

Taking leave of Mr. Tompkins and the lady, we walked another mile or so to pay a call on Mr. and Mrs. Malcolm Park, who, we had been informed, are the most ardent local archaeologists produced by the drought. The Parks told us that early every morning they tramp around the reservoir, picking things up. They showed us a box with their gleanings, which include a horseshoe, a plowshare, a bent wrought-iron nail, and fragments of pottery. Their most startling find, an automatic of recent manufacture, has been turned over to the Mount Kisco police. Several old revolvers have been found by others, Mr. and Mrs. Park told us, but no one is much surprised by them, because a former Mount Kisco chief of police used to get rid of confiscated weapons by dropping them into the reservoir from Pines Bridge. The Parks have discovered a number of Indian artifacts, among them arrowheads, a tomahawk, and a cylindrical stone that they think may have been used for tanning hides. They have also found plenty of clamshells. "There *are* freshwater clams," Mr. Park said, "but these shells look like salt-water ones. Our theory is that they're remnants of some high old clambakes."

Islands.

From *The New Yorker* in 1949 under the heading "Department of Amplification."

To the Editors, *The New Yorker*

Sirs:
Some time ago, under the heading, "Our Footloose Correspondents," you printed an article about Martinique, by T. E. Doremus, in which Mr. Doremus spoke of the high regard the Martiniquais have for Lafcadio Hearn, who dwelt on their island for two and a half years in the eighteen-eighties. He was responsible for my going there, in the winter of 1934. I came upon his "Martinique Sketches" in a branch of the New York Public Library, and immediately succumbed to romantic fever. Though the city of St. Pierre, whose population Hearn described as "fantastic, astonishing—a population out of the 'Thousand and One Nights,'" had been totally destroyed in the erup-

tion of Mt. Pelée, in 1902, I hoped to find some vestigial traces of "the most bizarre, the most picturesque and also the prettiest city of the Antilles." Standing by the rail of the French Line ship Columbie waiting to go ashore, I saw the rust-colored roofs of Fort-de-France under the arc of a double rainbow, and this motif was repeated in the façades of the stone houses and shops, which were painted in diagonal stripes of pink and green, and salmon and blue, faded and made chalky by the sun. The purser, learning that I meant to stay some time on the island, cautioned me against the hotels and recommended the Pension Gallia. Mr. Doremus does not mention this establishment, and I hope that it has not become extinct, like the fer-de-lance.

The Pension Gallia is situated in the center of the city, on a street that faced the harbor across the *savane*—a park of rough, unmowed grass. The rooms were clean and bare, there were no holes in the mosquito netting over my bed, and the *langouste* was excellent. The proprietress, Mme. Ti-ti-Man, was half mulatto and half Chinese. To her servants she was as hard as nails, and to me she was very kind. With the help of a French-English dictionary, she inquired at length about my family, warned me sternly against social disease, and saw to it that my excursions, by boat and by bus, were interesting and inexpensive. From the window of my room I had a clear view of the famous, rain-stained marble statue of the Empress Josephine in the *savane*, and of taxicabs waiting at the pier for a ship that wasn't due for two weeks. Though it was the dry season, it rained, briefly but hard, every morning at about twenty minutes after ten. I can still recall the heavy odors of the soft, lifeless air that belonged to the city, and the shape and position of the two mountains behind it.

Among the excursions that Mme. Ti-ti-Man arranged for me was one to the village of Trois Ilets, across the bay from Fort-de-France. She burst into my room one morning and ordered me to dress and hurry down to the pier, where a steamer was waiting to take people to Trois Ilets for nothing; in this way, she said, I could visit the birthplace of the Empress Josephine. It was a very hot day. I went on board in a white linen suit and a bright-green tie, and found myself surrounded by people dressed in mourning. The son of a rich sugar planter on Trois Ilets had been killed two days before in an automobile accident, and the boat was taking friends of the family across the bay to the funeral. Room was made for me to sit down, and the passengers couldn't have been more considerate of my feelings, or more polite. The funeral took place soon after we landed, and was magnificent. The hearse had black ostrich feathers on it, there were embroidered religious banners, and the mourners, following after the priests and acolytes, marched twice around the village square, and into the church. I wandered off across the fields in search of the abandoned sugar plantation that has been the early home of Napoleon Bonaparte's first wife. I never found it, chiefly because of an undue amount of rustling in the tall grass, which could just as well have been caused by fer-der-lances as by gophers.

There is a story that Martinique produced two concurrent empresses. The second—"The Veiled Empress"—was a cousin of Josephine's, whose name was Aimée du Buc de

Rivery. According to the custom for young girls of aristocratic family, she was sent to France for her education. In 1784, her parents arranged for her to return to Martinique on a sailing vessel, which left the harbor of Nantes, but never arrived at its port of destination. According to the somewhat dubious documents, the ship sprang a leak in the Bay of Biscay, and the passengers were transferred to a Spanish ship bound for Majorca. Just off the coast of that island, the Spanish vessel was attacked by buccaneers, and Aimée, in the words of the guidebook I found recently in our attic, "had the vexation of being taken captive by a Barbary Coast pirate, and after several more incidents, which the vulgar would consider trying for the beautiful Creole but which, in the order of her destiny, were only a step toward her future grandeur, she was placed in a harem, and soon, without doubt, her beauty and the advantages of an education *tres soigné* recommended her to the attention of the Sultan [of Turkey] then reigning, who made her his favorite Sultana." As the mother of Mahmud II, Aimée is suspected of having exerted considerable influence on Turkish foreign policy during the Napoleonic era and of having been partly responsible for the downfall of the ruler who behaved so badly towards her cousin. There is no statue of Aimée in Fort-de-France, possibly because the *savane* is small and would not gracefully accommodate two marble monuments.

IN MARTINIQUE, THE French colonists and the descendants of freed African slaves, by repeated intermarrying, have produced a thoroughly French Negro. The Martiniquais can create an illusion of style—out of rags, if necessary—that sets him apart from the natives of the British West Indies. During carnival season, which began on Twelfth Night and lasted through Ash Wednesday, it was never easy to tell who was in costume and who was not. The fishermen frequently wore their old felt hats upside down, in the shape of tricornes, and dressed in colors that went well with the color of their skin. The old women were faithful to the traditional dress, which is beautiful. The young women preferred cotton print dresses from France, but, like their mothers and grandmothers, still wore turbines of madras, imported from India and sold in the shop that called itself the Hundred Thousand Handkerchiefs. The carnival went on, or didn't go on, according (I suppose) to the religious calendar, with the revelers masked and disguised as clowns, cowboys, or Alsatians, or as themselves. Some nights, there was dance music, and a big man wearing a trident and hideous mask and a headdress of goats' hide, cows' horns, bells, bits of mirrors, and pieces of money led a pack of fifty or sixty little boys through the dark streets and along a canal, acting out a fable that had to do with the Devil crossing the river. The music I heard standing outside a dance hall by the canal had been, I was told, composed in the doomed city of St. Pierre and since handed down from musician to musician. Its pattern consisted of a single phrase repeated raucously by one instrument after another or by all of them, long past the point of endurance. Other nights, the city was quiet, the sky drenched with stars, and the only diversion was supplied by the fishermen who follow the narrow strip of sand at the water's edge, talking softly to themselves and drawing their nets up out of the sea.

At the time of my visit, three Americans were living permanently on Martinique: an aged volcanologist in charge of the seismographic station on a slope of Mt. Pelée, a Ford dealer who had married into one of the wealthy old French families, and the American Consul. I stayed only a month on the island, but a month on Martinique is easily the equivalent of a year on the mainland of North America. Before I left, I went to St. Pierre on a coastal steamer that worked its way around the island. The modern city was a little more than a row of buildings along the waterfront. The streets leading away from the harbor were lined on both sides with houses that had no roofs, windows, or doors, and mangoes and banana trees were growing in what once had to be in the halls and parlors. Mt. Pelée looked calm and wicked. In the course of an eighteen-mile bus ride back over the mountains, through what must surely be some of the world's most impressive scenery, we were delayed a dozen times by punctures and blowouts. The last stop occurred along about dusk. The driver got out his pump and vulcanizing patches, and I went down a winding path with a Negro taxi-driver and another passenger, an Irish priest from Boston, in search of something to eat. We came upon a lonely hut, where the Negro persuaded a native woman to feed us. We had cooked breadfruit and wine, and in such a remote place, at that uneasy hour, I kept feeling the weight of my wallet. The wine taking effect, we indulged in a crescendo of international compliments, and when the bus horn sounded, the taxi-driver rose, took out an enormous roll of franc notes, and, over the priest's and my protests, paid for all three of us. In this act of generosity, as I remember, the honor of France was involved.

Reporter at Large: The King of St. David's (1940).

THE JEALOUSLY GUARDED Victorian charm of Bermuda is being threatened—not by automobiles, but by planes. The planes are not Hitler's; they belong to the United States, and will be attached to the naval and airplane base which we recently acquired there.

During the last war, the United States was lent White's Island, in Hamilton Harbour, as a base for submarine chasers, and when peace was declared, handed it back again. Bermudians assumed that the base this time would merely involve the lease of one of the numerous islands in Great Sound, through which steamships pass on the way into the harbor, and the use of the neighboring waters, but after a brief visit, the United States Army board of inspection asked for several islands in the Sound and a wide corridor across, what is called "the mainland." This corridor would cut Bermuda in two for the next ninety-nine years and make necessary the resettlement of about fifteen hundred people.

The colonial government, in great distress, sent two representatives to Washington. According to the *Royal Gazette & Colonist Daily*, they explained to the late

Lord Lothian "the extent to which the acceptance of the scheme would prejudice the future amenities of the Colony," and offered an alternative scheme which has proved acceptable to the United States. The details of this plan were announced in Bermuda late in November.

The United States has been granted almost as extensive privileges as it originally asked for, but our military activities are now confined to the east end of the islands, where fewer inhabitants are affected and where it is hoped that our planes will do the tourist business less harm. The land turned over to the United States totals approximately five hundred and ten acres, of which three hundred and thirty acres are on St. David's Island and forty on St. George's Island. Long Bird Island, Cooper's Island, Nonsuch Island (where Dr. Beebe conducted his first experiment with the bathysphere), Castle Island, and ten other small islands are also included in the lease. American Army engineers have received permission to blast channels in Castle Harbour which is now about as deep as a bathtub; to build a new bridge at Ferry Point high enough for large bombing planes to taxi under; and to tear down the Causeway, which is two miles long and has for the last seventy years connected the island of St. George with the mainland. A new causeway, an extension of the North Shore Road, will take its place.

The devisers of the present plan passed up Vincent Astor's place on Sr. George, but a number of Americans will have to abandon their property, among them Dr. Beebe, George Walters, Beale W. Fuller, and Mrs. Marshall Field. One or two Bermudians are unfortunate enough to have leased land in this area on which they were growing Easter-lily bulbs, but the really serious hardship will be worked upon the residents of St. David's Island, who are extremely poor and cannot even imagine living in any other place.

Sometime in the last half of the seventeenth century, fifty male Pequot Indians from Massachusetts Bay and their chief were exiled to Bermuda and sold into slavery there. Many of these Indians were purchased by a landowner on St. David's. Since they had no wives, they intermarried with Negro slaves. About the same time, Oliver Cromwell, having subdued Ireland, impulsively shipped fifty troublesome, red-headed Irishmen to Bermuda, and they too ended up on St. David's. A great many of the present inhabitants of the island show obvious characteristics of all three races. Though inbred, they are independent, courageous, devout people, with little interest in money and none whatever in the rest of Bermuda.

Their island was accessible only by boat until a bridge was built between St. David's Island and St. George's Island in 1934. It didn't make much difference to the St. David's Islanders. "If God had intended St. David's to be part of the mainland," I heard one of them say, "he'd have made it that way in the beginning. But he meant it to be an island, and he meant the people on the island to earn their living by fishing and pilotage."

The most celebrated person on St. David's is a very old man—Captain Henry Mortimer Fox. No one ever calls him that. He is known either as Tommy Fox or as the King of St. David's. Nearly all books on Bermuda contain an account of his homemade oven, his fifty or a hundred reticent cats, and his descent into the belly of a sperm whale for the purpose of corroborating Jonah's tale. According to one of the travel books, "The Story of Bermuda," by Hudson Strode, Mr. Fox's father piloted English ships through the blockade to Confederate ports during the Civil War, made $3,500 a trip, and invested it in land on St. David's. His son is the largest landowner in Bermuda. The American naval base will absorb practically all of his two hundred acres, including the beautiful, secluded beach at Ruth's Bay.

I DECIDED TO go to Ruth's Bay, after the plans for the naval base were announced, take a picnic lunch, and have a swim. The last time I had been there was the summer before the war broke out, and I remembered it with affection. I persuaded Mrs. Fred Trimingham, a widowed American woman who married into one of the old Bermuda families, to go with me.

It was nine-thirty in the morning and the sun was shining like summer when we started out from Waterville, Mrs. Trimingham's guest house in Paget. From there to the lighthouse on St. David's is fourteen miles—two hours at least by carriage. Although December is an off season for gardens in Bermuda, hibiscus hedges and the bougainvillea were in bloom all along the way, and poinsettia fifteen feet high. Our driver had the incredible name of Robert Sodagreen.

We found the first signs of change when we reached the Causeway. Half a dozen members of the United

States Army Corps of Engineers were there ahead of us, with range rods, surveying instruments, and strips of bright-red cloth. On Long Bird Island, across which the Causeway leads, we passed the only pretentious place in the condemned area—the uncompleted estate of William Marcus Greve, a former New Yorker who is now a naturalized citizen of Liechtenstein. A scrap of red cloth was fastened to its entrance gate. The estate, which would have cost $200,000 to complete, will be levelled off to a height of eight feet above the harbour and used as a landing field. In her husband's lifetime, Mrs. Trimingham said, she had often gone fishing at St. David's and in that way had got to know a good many of the islanders. She was particularly fond of old Mrs. Tommy Fox and had brought along a basket of fruit for her. Since Mrs. Fox's house is not on the main road, we stopped at the drawbridge connecting St. George's and St. David's and asked the way. The man tending the bridge turned out to be one of Tommy Fox's grandsons, and gave us fairly simple directions. When we spoke about the naval base, he shook his head. "I'm one of the lucky ones," he said. "My house is on the north side of the island."

As soon as you cross the bridge, the surroundings are so different that Bermudians insist on referring to St. David's as primitive. Actually, it has a soft, rolling landscape made up of pastures and lily fields, groves of wind-twisted cedars, and glimpses of beautiful blue water. Some of the houses are shacks, but many are well built and of stone. The island generally is as it must have been all during the last century.

As we drove along, Mrs. Trimingham pointed out certain distinguishing marks of the St. David's Islander. The men are barefoot, often as not, and wear faded trousers rolled to the knee, a ragged shirt, a vest, and a battered old hat. They are always tanned, they hold themselves well, and when they walk they lift their feet rather as if they were going through high weeds.

The only good road goes from the bridge to the St. George's ferry, and it has a fork running up to the lighthouse. As soon as we turned off the main road, we were in trouble; the road quickly became wagon tracks and then bright-green grass. We came upon a woman feeding her chickens, and our driver stopped to ask her if the road was passable. She thought the carriage might make it part of the way, but then there was a hill, quite a steep hill, with no place on the other side to turn around. We decided to take the basket of fruit and go the rest of the way to Tommy Fox's house on foot.

"I'm a Fox too," the woman told us. "My house belongs to Tommy Fox."

Mrs. Trimingham asked if she were going to lose it.

"Yes," the woman said, "We'll have to go. Very hard."

When she had finished feeding her chickens she went with us part of the way. We passed a man hoeing in a small field. "Mr. Hollis is going ahead with his sweet potatoes," the woman said cheerfully.

At the foot of the steep hill she left us. We climbed to the top, and on the other side we looked down on the roof of the large stone house where Foxes have lived for a century and a quarter. It is two stories high and as substantial as any old house I have seen in Bermuda. Beyond it a meadow sloped down to the shore, where two dozen Bermudian Negroes in khaki uniforms were drilling with rifles, and beyond them were fishing nets spread out in the sun to dry.

The path went down past a big tree, and on a bench under the tree three men were sitting—two of them old and one a middle-aged man whom Mrs. Trimingham recognized as a son of Tommy Fox. I knew him as the man who used to keep the bathhouses at Ruth's Bay. There are five or six of them in a row and it used to be a shilling if you could pay, and if you couldn't pay, why, you could use the bathhouses for nothing. Mrs. Trimingham told me that so few Americans go to Ruth's Bay now it is no longer worthwhile for him to stay there. He looked unwell. Mrs. Trimingham asked if his mother was in, and he said that she was and that she was feeling very bad about losing their home.

"What bothers me," one of the old men said, "is that we don't know when we're to go. We're waiting for our rent notice, you might say."

"If they find me a home, I'll be satisfied," the other old man said. "Many people over there's been burnt out. The Americans can't help it. I mean to say, they *have* to take it. America's trying to help England. They're the only two English-speaking countries and they have to stand by each other. I served my country for thirty-eighty years and my son is serving her now. My heart's with my King and Crown."

"They'll have to find us a place where we'll be together," the first old man said. "People here do a lot of going back and forth."

EVENTUALLY THE PATH led around the house to the front door, which was wide open. Mrs. Trimingham and I walked into what was clearly both dining and sitting room. Across the ceiling there were beams of highly polished dark wood. The room was plain and bare and very clean. On the sideboards were family portraits, china, two coronation mugs (one of Edward VIII and the other of George and Elizabeth), and a bowl of tropical fruit of a kind neither of us had ever seen before. Mrs. Trimingham called out and a large, elderly, nearsighted woman appeared. For a moment she didn't know what to make of us. Then she recognized Mrs. Trimingham and kissed her. When she had looked into the basket, her face lit up with pleasure. Mrs. Trimingham explained that we were going to Ruth's Bay.

"Mr. Fox always calls it his front dooryard," the old woman said. Her face grew sad. "Ain't it awful!" she said, turning to me. "It seems like an invasion, what I've read of them. America's been very kind. I always said if anyone had to take the island, I'd rather it was the Americans. They've always been more congenial, you know." Two cats walked in from out-of-doors. "Mr. Fox doesn't seem to realize," she said to Mrs. Trimingham. "He's worried, I know, but he doesn't talk about it much." Far from being the shy animals described in Bermuda travel books, the cats walked under my legs and disappeared into the depths of the house. "I don't know where to go or what to do. My sister has a house, but the bedrooms are upstairs and I don't know as I'm fit. It's concrete, you know, and there's the dampness." She turned to me and smiled. "I never cared for airplanes. I always used to say they were Satan's invention."

I asked about the fruit on the sideboard, and she told me that it was sugar apples, which are so uncommon in Bermuda that, although Mrs. Trimingham remembered her husband's speaking of them, she had never seen any.

It was twelve-thirty when we stood up to go. Mrs. Fox asked us to stay for dinner and, after we refused, told us that Mr. Fox was with the men in the potato patch and that if we walked along the shore, we'd probably meet him coming home. I ran back over the hill, past the old men, and told the carriage-driver to meet us at Ruth's Bay. By the time I returned to the house, Mrs. Fox had brought out a bottle of English ginger wine and two green glasses with clear stems. As I was uncorking the bottle for her, she touched one of the wine-glasses to the other, and the delicate ring hung on the still air in the house.

On our way to the Bay we saw the King of St. David's coming along the shore, as his wife thought we would. He was a tall, erect, handsome old man. He had a blond fifteen-year-old boy with him, and as soon as they noticed us, they veered off. But then Mr. Fox recognized Mrs. Trimingham and came toward us across the sand. "I don't always look like a pig," he said when she introduced me to him.

The apology was unnecessary and perhaps insincere. He had shoes on and was wearing khaki trousers, a clean shirt, an old tweed vest, and a straw hat which had taken its shape from use. Under his collar was a clean bandage; he has for years been afflicted with a peculiar bleeding at the back of his neck. His features were aristocratic and his eyes full of humor. His gray mustache was stained with tobacco juice and the ends seemed to have been blown into his mouth by the sea wind.

Mrs. Trimingham explained that we had left some fruit at his house and were now heading for Ruth's Bay.

"My bay's gone," he said quietly. "They've taken it. I wouldn't have minded a proportion, but they've taken the whole bloody lot. The Furness Line wanted it, but I said no. My father left me this land, and what my father gave me I don't sell. I asked 'em did they ever hear of King Ahab and the vineyard Naboth's father left him, and they said they didn't think they had. You don't know about anything, I told 'em." He turned to me. "You know the story?" I said I did, but he told it anyway, with relish. When he had finished, Mrs. Trimingham asked about his health—he will be eighty the fifteenth of February.

"The last week my head ain't been so good, but I ain't worrying. They can't make me leave my home. Where'd I go? Where'd I get a home like that? Where'd I put my things?" He looked past us to the house we had just left. "I'd give 'em part," he said. "America's the only friend England's got since France quit on 'em. But they want to take my orchards—my apple trees and my banana trees that I been puttin' up fences for and fightin' hurricanes. They'll pay me money, but money ain't no good. If you're as rich as Rothschild, you can't live outdoors. And they didn't leave me a place where I could lay my boat."

There was an awkward silence; then Mrs. Trimingham suggested that we were keeping him from his lunch.

"I don't mind when I eat," he said. "I come home and my wife says, 'Where you been all time? It's nearly two o'clock.' I says what difference it make if it was four." He laughed then, and stepped aside for us to pass.

THE PATH ALONG the shore led us shortly to Ruth's Bay. We found driver and carriage there, and the horse un-hitched and eating grass. We chose a place under some cedar trees and unpacked the lunch. While we were eating, a Negro, barefoot and bare to the waist, came down to the beach and moved a cow that he apparently imagined was too close to our picnic grounds. The bath-houses were on one side of us, the lighthouse hill at our backs. The bay was as clear as drinking water and there was seaweed along the white sand. Cooper's Island and Nonsuch were quite close. They are soon to become sites of storehouses for ammunition and high explosives, but at present one of them is in use as a reformatory for boys; the other is inhabited mostly by birds.

After lunch, I left Mrs. Trimingham reading a book under a tree and went for a swim. Toward the middle of the afternoon, as I was walking along the shore, I met Mr. Fox again, carrying a brown paper bag. "They call me King—you've heard that, haven't you?" he asked as I turned back with him. "That's because I don't associate with Tom, Dick, and Harry." Then he told me how he had once met a woman who asked if she should turn left to go to Ruth's Bay. "'Turn left or right, whichever you please,' I told her. 'It all belongs to me.'"

A rowboat was drawn up on the shore beside the bathhouses. Mr. Fox sat down in one end and offered me the other. From his vest pocket he drew out a triangular Masonic watch, wrapped in wax paper, which he wanted to show me. An American to whom he had given some whaling relics had sent it to him, he said. He asked me my name, and when I told him, he said that there was a street by that name in New Bedford. That started him talking about his father's trips there and about the whaling ships that used to stop at St. David's Island to pick up men for the long voyage around the Horn. Finally he gave me a temperance lecture.

AT THREE O'CLOCK, I saw the driver hitching his horse to the carriage and stood up to go. Mr. Fox went up the hill with me. Mrs. Trimingham was waiting beside the carriage, and when he saw her he held out his paper bag. "My wife sent you some sugar apples and she said not to eat 'em till they get soft," he said. Mrs. Trimingham tried to thank him, but he changed the subject. As we got into the carriage, he asked how long I was going to be in Bermuda. I explained that I didn't know—perhaps till after Christmas.

"Won't be much Christmas this year," he said. "Most years there is. Go from house to house here, and there ain't nobody too poor to offer you something. This year I don't know where we'll be. I don't mind for myself. I could live in a shack. But I got a wife and a sick boy. I'm goin' to ask 'em to let me live in my house. I'm goin' to plead with 'em." He stepped back from the carriage. "Well," he said, "come again, since you're goin' to be here till Christmas. If I'm not dead. I'll be here. I'm never anywhere but here."

PART II

NOTES AND REMARKS ON WRITING

The Impulse Toward Autobiographical Fiction
A speech given at the University of Illinois in March of 1963

AN AUTOBIOGRAPHICAL NOVELIST is the kind of man who would go to the funeral of somebody who had been like a father to him, and worry all through the one-hundred and third psalm because he has absent-mindedly worn brown shoes with a black suit. "As for man," the minister said solemnly, "his days are as grass; As a flower of the field, so he flourisheth. For the wind passeth over it, and it is gone. And the place thereof shall know it no more . . ." The novelist heard him, all right. But were people staring at his shoes?

I don't mean by this that he is a person who cares about his clothes. Or that he is too wrapped up in himself to be capable of human feelings. Or that he is conceited. What is he, then? An egoist, of course. He will hear what you are saying, and he will even be interested in it. And in you. But the finer shades of his interest are always for what is going on in his own mind. He is profoundly and faithfully, year in and year out, interested in himself—in his own psychological makeup, his own character, the drama—both internal and external—of his own life, as it is played out with himself as both the leading actor and a substantial part of the audience. By upbringing alone, we are led to conclude that this is not very attractive. Even without the upbringing, it's unattractive, egoism, but those qualities a person cannot

help having there is no point in blaming him for. The autobiographical writer was born an egoist, and will pass out
of life more interested in his own dying than in the grief
of anyone at his deathbed. By rights he should die alone,
with nobody to grieve over him, but he probably won't.
We know, anyway, that Marcel Proust didn't. Or Samuel
Butler. There will be somebody. Probably a faithful servant.
But let us consider those brown shoes. He cared enough
about the dead man to get there. He didn't go to the wrong
place, or arrive by taxi just as the mourners were coming
out of the church, or think the funeral was the next day
instead of the day it actually was. The affection was genuine, and absentminded though he is, he got himself there.
As a matter of fact, he was fifteen minutes early. Suppose
we go back to the moment of his hurried dressing, before
breakfast that morning. Here a choice of interpretation is
offered. Either you believe that absentmindedness is that
and nothing more, or you are ready to believe that through
absentminded behavior one betrays feelings that one ordinarily conceals from oneself and from other people. It is
quite possible that the brown shoes are a protest. The novelist—from now on I am going to refer to him as George
Holland—didn't like funerals. He also didn't like death—
his own or anyone else's. And he is always slightly out of
step with his social environment. If it had been a cocktail
party instead of a funeral, there would have been something
about his dress that would have been inappropriate for that
occasion also. He would have neglected to change his shirt.
Or he would have needed a haircut. The truth is that the
autobiographical writer is nearly always subversive.

Samuel Butler wrote *The Way of All Flesh* as an act of sabotage. If there was one thing that was dear to Victorian England it was its myopic view of family life. This was not dear to Butler. He thought that fathers were very often tyrannical, that mothers were not to be trusted, that the rights of children were not respected, that family life was more shocking than beautiful. From this distance, from the place where we are now, the Victorian family does look rather like the fraud Butler said it was. In any case, he called the shots for the first time, and so gave children a weapon against their parents that is, I believe, in use even today.

As a small child, in the year 1918, Mary McCarthy left Seattle, with her mother and father and two brothers. Either before they got on the train or after they had boarded it, her parents contracted the Spanish influenza. The conductor tried to put them off the train, but her father objected strenuously, and they were allowed to proceed to their destination, which was, I believe, Minneapolis. Her father and mother were removed from the train on stretchers, and died within twenty-four hours. The children were handed over to their grandparents, who decided that it was wiser not to tell them what had happened to their father and mother. It was many years before they found out. Meanwhile, they were treated with extraordinary cruelty. All this is told in a story called "Yonder Peasant, Who is He?" which no doubt many of you have read. Speaking of this story, Miss McCarthy says: "It is, primarily, an angry indictment of privilege for its treatment of the underprivileged, a single breathless, voluble speech on the subject of human indifference. We orphan children were not responsible for being orphans, but we were treated as if we were and as if being orphans were a crime we had committed. Read 'poor' for 'orphan' throughout and you get a kind of allegory or broad social satire on the theme of wealth and poverty. The anger was generalized anger, which held up my grandparents as specimens of unfeeling behavior."

The French aristocracy that Proust described so lovingly and with such exhaustive detail is in the end exposed for what it really is—a society without moral standards, without intelligence, and without feeling; a sham. After reading *The Great Gatsby* you can never meet a very rich person without feeling the creeps.

Ordinarily one thinks of a subversive person as someone bent on changing the way things are and bringing about a better world—at least, better to his way of thinking. But the autobiographical novelist is seldom interested in the future, and he is enslaved by the past. All change is like an illness. It is a deprivation from which he can never recover.

I once met somebody who had known Willa Cather—a man who works in a publisher's office—and I began to question him about her, because she led a secluded life in her later years, and saw very few people. As he was telling me about her, I suddenly interrupted him to ask "What made her a writer?" He looked at me oddly and said, "Why, what makes anyone a writer—deprivation, of course." And then he apologized for being tactless.

It goes without saying that whatever the standard for normal behavior is, all writers are abnormal and peculiar.

Consider how Fielding ran through his wife's money. Jane Austen and Flaubert never married. Walt Whitman told the most terrible whoppers. Henry James could not ask the way to the corner drugstore in a way that anybody could understand him. Joyce was ungrateful. Turgenev as a young man was a physical coward. Dostoyevsky was a compulsive gambler. As for what went on in the Tolstoy household, it was almost beyond belief. And these are the *respectable* writers. I won't even go into the other kind. But I think we can assume that it does not make a writer any less queer to have his interest turned inward upon himself, and to care so passionately about the past.

In the Chicago Art Institute, in a corridor on the first floor, there is an old-fashioned and I think very beautiful statue by Lorado Taft. It is called the *Solitude of the Soul*. It consists of four figures, two women and two men, all emerging in slightly different attitudes from one central block of marble. In the most moving way, one hand of each figure touches a hand or a shoulder of the next, but their eyes do not meet, their faces are turned away from each other, they look inward. A great deal of the time, so do we. Regrets, daydreams, memories, secrets, secret places of withdrawal, are the very climate in which our matter-of-fact, transparent, busy, ordinary life is conducted. In the *Solitude of the Soul*, everybody is queer. On the other hand, every affliction—and queerness is a symptom of trouble, of affliction—seems to bring with it some compensating talent. Blind people not only have, as a rule, very active hearing, they have two spots on their cheeks that act as organs of seeing. So the autobiographical writer has an inner photographic plate that is highly sensitive to sights, sounds, smells, colors, taste, touch, and so on. He also has an unusually retentive memory. Wolcott Gibbs speaks somewhere of having been at a party with Thurber when they were both young men. Thurber was bored. He was quite easily bored. He sat off in a corner the whole evening and didn't talk to anybody or pay any attention to what was going on. Ten years later, to Gibbs's astonishment, Thurber wrote a story in which that rather dull party was recorded down to the last merciless detail.

The processes of memory begin, I suppose, as soon as a child is born, but somewhere amnesia sets in, and children have to begin remembering all over again—usually from when they are four or five or six years old. A writer I know remembers vividly—so vividly that there is no question of its being based on something he heard from someone else—he remembers being taken out to a wheat field, about fifty miles from here, by his father, to see an airplane go up. The plane belongs to the Wright brothers, and in those days most people had never seen an airplane in the air. So it was a major event. It was a hot afternoon in August, and the wheat field was full of people who were walking around, and tramping down the farmer's wheat. They waited and they waited. They waited all afternoon and nothing happened. The plane didn't go up. The writer thought that he was four years old when this happened. When he was in his forties, he happened to mention the incident to his father, who informed him that he was not four when this happened, but two and a half. With writers, and particularly with autobiographical writers, the amnesia seems to be only partial.

The train that Anna Karenina threw herself under the wheels of was not a real train—that is to say, not an actual train that Tolstoy remembered. I am not sure that I could have stood it if it had been. It's bad enough having her killed by an imaginary train. Here is a real train, remembered by another writer [Nabokov] from his childhood: ". . . The firs and swamps of northwestern Russia sped by, and on the following day gave way to German pine barrens and heather. Wearing a checked traveling cap and gray cotton gloves, my father sat reading a book in his compartment. At a collapsible table, my mother and I played a card game called *durachki*. Although it was still broad daylight, our cards, a glass, and on a different plane, the locks of a suitcase were reflected in the window. Through forest and field, and in sudden ravines, and among scuttling cottages, those discarnate gamblers kept steadily playing on for steadily sparkling stakes.

"'Haven't you had enough? Aren't you tired?' my mother would ask, and then be lost in thought as she slowly shuffled the cards. The door of the compartment was open and I could see the corridor window, where the wires—six thin black wires—were doing their best to slant up, to ascend skyward, despite the lightning blows dealt them by one telegraph pole after another, but just as all six, in a triumphant swoop of pathetic elation, were about to reach the top of the window, a particularly vicious blow would bring them down, as low as they had ever been, and they would have to start all over again."

Just as writing, those telegraph poles could hardly be improved on. But there is something else that is not pure description. What could have been merely a visual impression has the quality of an emotional experience. Of a kind of disaster. Why? Why should this visual impression, which you and I and everybody who has ever gone on a train journey can recognize, have such a weight of sadness? Something must have happened to him, we say to ourselves, and this is just what the writer meant us to think.

Let us get on with the journey: We have arrived at the stage of train-sickness. ". . . The wide-windowed dining car, a vista of chaste bottles of mineral water, mitre-folded napkins, and dummy chocolate bars (whose wrappers— Cailler, Kohler, and so forth—enclosed nothing but wood), would be perceived at first as a cool haven beyond a consecution of reeling blue corridors, but as the meal progressed toward its last fatal course, one would keep catching the car in the act of being recklessly sheathed, lurching waiters and all, in the landscape, while the landscape itself went through a complex system of motion, the daytime moon stubbornly keeping abreast of one's own plate, the distant meadows opening fanwise, the near trees sweeping up on invisible swings toward the track, a parallel rail line suddenly committing suicide by anastomosis, a bank of grass rising, rising, rising, until the little witness of mixed velocities was made to disgorge its portion of *omelette aux confitures de fraises* . . . .

"It was night, however, that the Compagnie Internationale des Wagons-Lits et des Grand Express Europeans lived up to the magic of its name. From my bed under my brother's bunk (Was he asleep? Was he there at all?), in the semi-darkness of our compartment, I watched things, and parts of things, and shadows, and sections of shadows cautiously moving about and getting nowhere. The woodwork gently creaked and crackled. Near the door that led to the toilet, a dim garment on a peg, and higher up, the tassel of the blue, bivalved night light swung rhythmically. It was hard to correlate those halting approaches, that hooded stealth, with the headlong rush of the outside night, which I knew *was* rushing by, spark-streaked, illegible . . . .

"A change in the speed of the train sometimes interrupted the current of my sleep. Slow lights were stalking by; each, in passing, investigated the same chink, and then a luminous compass measured the shadows. Presently, the train stopped with a long-drawn Westinghousian sigh. Something (my brother's spectacles, as it proved the next day) fell from above. It was marvelously exciting to move to the foot of one's bed, with part of the bedclothes following, in order to undo cautiously the catch of the window shade, which could be made to slide only halfway up, impeded as it was by the edge of the upper berth.

"Like moons around Jupiter, hail moths revolved about a lone lamp. A dismembered newspaper stirred on a bench. Somewhere on the train one could hear muffled noises, somebody's comfortable cough. There was nothing particularly interesting in the portion of station platform before me, and still I could not tear myself away from it until it departed of its own accord . . ."

I trust that you noticed that dismembered newspaper. Objects have never been immune to sudden destruction, but in our age, now that we are not immune either, objects are asked to share our terror of annihilation with us—to go through it consciously, so to speak, so we won't lack company. "Like Jupiter and his moons"—all childhood is in that optical transference of the ordinary and the small into the planetary immensity. And there is of course a philosophic support for the idea that the station departed of its own accord. But all this is secondary to the emotional communication. While you are learning about the train journey you are also, half unconsciously, drawing some important conclusions about the man who is remembering it. He would not have described those telegraph wires with such sympathy, such empathy, if he himself had not, at some time between that actual journey and the moment when he sat down to write about it, have had his own hopes struck down again and again, by periodic blows of fate. In the description of the dining car, one finds the words "haven", "last fatal course", "recklessly", "stubborn", "committing suicide." Taken superficially, and individually, they are gently humorous. What they add up to is that life has been all but too much for the writer, that his happiness has hung by a thread, that the thread has sometimes broken, that he knows what it means to turn one's face to the wall.

In a collection of literary essays called "The Art of Fiction," Mr. Somerset Maugham says: ". . . God, fate, chance, whatever you like to call the mystery that governs men's lives, is a poor storyteller; and it is the business, and the right, of the novelist to correct the improbabilities of brute fact." This statement makes George Holland froth at the mouth.

He believes in the mysterious importance and meaning of actual events—of, in fact, everything that happens.

In Samuel Butler's notebooks there is an entry five lines long, referring to Ernest Pontifex, the hero of "The Way of All Flesh," who as everybody knows was modelled on Butler himself. "It cost me a great deal to make Ernest play Beethoven and Mendelssohn. I did it simply for the sake of pleasing the crowd. As a matter of fact he played only Handel and the early Italians and old English composers—but Handel most of all." This is, of course, absurd; the non-musical reader couldn't care less whether Ernest played Beethoven or Handel. But it is interesting that Butler cared, that he was reluctant to depart from the facts, and that when he did, it troubled him afterward. It troubles George Holland, too, and it troubles him a good deal more, for the simple reason that he has read Freud and Butler had not. This is not to say that George Holland has swallowed Freud lock, stock and barrel. And when he resorts to clinical psychology to explain a character, he does his best to avoid jargon, and to keep from sitting down complacently in the analyst's chair. The case history is one thing and art, the art of fiction, is another, and they don't mix. What the contemporary novelist owes to Freud is the realization that no detail of what happens to us is trivial, because at any moment, through the play of association, it may become central to our whole experience, the combination that unlocks the safe and hands over the otherwise unexplainable mystery.

Far from being a poor storyteller, life, looked at carefully, is so full of exquisite detail, of plot, of suspense, of ideas, of architectural structure, of everything that goes

to make a successful novel, that to do anything but reproduce what happened to the best of one's ability is to
be lacking in literary intelligence. Or so George Holland
believes. This is an extreme position, of course. What he
says when you back him into a corner is that the writer
should know what cannot be improved upon, especially
when it is handed to him on a platter.

This is not the same thing as saying that the imagination of the writer should surrender its authority to the
outward form of actual events. Also, a person trying his
best to recount a dream inevitably offers you a mixture of
the real dream and something that he invented while he
was talking to you. Just as what is called "pure fiction" has
always had some element of the autobiographical in it, so
autobiographical fiction is never without some degree of
pure invention. The innate storyteller cannot be prevented
from adding a touch here and an arabesque there, even
when he doesn't mean to do it, because they are part of
his tradition and trade. Ten years after a writer has finished writing an autobiographical novel, he won't be entirely sure what is invented and what is literally true. And
in telling about an experience that he has written about
he may innocently substitute an invention for a fact. This
doesn't matter to anybody, and there is a sense in which
it doesn't even matter from the point of view of telling
the truth, because every invention also means something,
though what it means can easily be hidden by and from
the person who has thought it up.

There are, however, certain disadvantages that come
from working so directly from life. There is, first of all, the

law on the subject of libel and invasion of privacy. There are social pressures—what the society of any given time thinks it is suitable for a writer to write about. Here, of course, society and the artist part company, since one is interested in the truth as he sees it and the other, generally speaking, in as much of the truth as it is expedient to recognize and no more.

There are also personal checks, moral scruples, the fear of inflicting harm on living people. There is, further, the danger, the trap, implicit in the use of the mirror. Sometimes the writer and the reader draw apart, because the writer is looking with satisfaction at himself and the reader, catching him at it, is amused, or embarrassed for him, or both. And with drama that is to such a considerable extent inward—cause and effect, feelings, attitudes, associations, memories, outweighing action in the physical world—the writer has to take into consideration the reader's instinctive requirements, what is and what is not worth being a witness to. Because the reader has, after all, a novel going on inside *him*, also, night and day, and turns his attention from it only in the expectation of something more interesting, more instructive, more profound, or more entertaining.

All this being so, why is so much of contemporary fiction autobiographical? What's wrong with *Tom Jones* and *Pride and Prejudice* and *Vanity Fair* and *The Ordeal of Richard Feveral* and *The Secret Agent*? The answer is "Nothing." They are perfect, or as near as one can reasonably expect a novel to be. But prose fiction shows a tendency not to want to repeat itself, and so a triumph by one writer makes other writers turn away towards something that is still undone. In this perpetual turning away, skills become lost, or go out of fashion. It used to be part of the equipment of any practicing novelist that he could do a romantic heroine. For example: "Her bare arms and shoulders were white and beautiful; the materials of her dress, a mixture, he supposed, of silk and crepe, were of a silvery gray so artfully composed as to give an impression of warm splendor; and round her neck she wore a collar of large old emeralds, the green tone of which was repeated, at other points of her apparel, in embroidery, in enamel, in satin, in substances and textures vaguely rich. Her head, extremely fair and exquisitely festal, was like a happy fancy, a notion of the antique, on an old precious medal, some silver coin of the Renaissance; while her slim lightness and brightness, her gaiety, her expression, her decision, contributed to an effect that might have been felt by a poet as half mythological and half conventional. He could have compared her to a goddess still partly engaged in a morning cloud, or to a sea-nymph waist high in the summer surge." There you are. Nothing to it. Only, as it happens, nobody can do this particular trick anymore.

What you get, instead, is something like this: "Mlle. Albertine has gone . . . . The words had expressed themselves in my heart in the form of an anguish so keen that I would not be able to endure it for any length of time. And so what I had supposed to mean nothing to me was the only thing in my whole life. How ignorant we are of ourselves. The first thing to be done was to make my anguish cease at once. Tender towards myself as my mother had been toward my dying grandmother, I said to myself with that anxiety which we feel to prevent a person whom we love from suffering, 'Be patient for just a moment, we shall find something to take the pain away, don't fret, we are not going to allow you to suffer like this.'" In the first instance, the reader's feelings are appealed to. And there is not one moment in which the writer is thinking about himself. In the second instance, it is the reader's understanding and memory. He is not asked to fall in love with Albertine, but only to remember, and, remembering, to perceive the accuracy of the writer's observations. In case you are thinking that this is not an accomplishment of the first order, take a look—that is to say, listen to how Henry Fielding deals with a similar situation, in *Tom Jones*:

"Many contending passions were raised in our hero's mind by this letter; but the tender prevailed at last over the indignant and the irascible, and a flood of tears came seasonably to his assistance, and possibly prevented his misfortunes from either turning his head or bursting his heart.

"He grew, however, soon ashamed of indulging this remedy; and starting up, he cried, 'Well, then, I will give Mr. Allworthy the only instance he requires of my obedience. I will go this moment—but wither?—why, let Fortune direct; since there is no other who thinks it of any consequence what becomes of this wretched person, it shall be a matter of equal indifference to myself. Shall I alone regard what no other—Ha! have I not reason to think there *is* another?—one whose value is above that of the whole world!—I may, I must imagine my Sophia is not indifferent to what becomes of me. Shall I then leave this only friend—and such a friend? Shall I not stay with her? Where—how *can* I stay with her? Have I any hopes of ever seeing her, though she was as desirous as myself, without exposing her to the wrath of her father, and to what purpose? Can I think of soliciting such a creature to consent to her own ruin? Shall I indulge any passion of mine at such a price? Shall I lurk about this country like a thief, with such intentions? No, I disclaim, I detest the thought. Farewell, Sophia; farewell, most lovely, most beloved—' Here passion stopped his mouth and found vent in his eyes."

The difference in the two passages is not a matter of our taste as compared with the taste of the eighteenth century; Tom Jones is not dated. It is simply that one writer's strength is the other writer's weakness, though both books are masterpieces of fiction.

In exchange for those accomplishments which he has either been unable to master or turned his back on, what does the autobiographical writer bring to contemporary fiction?

By tradition, the novelist has tended to think of himself as holding a mirror up to life. Turning all the way around, the autobiographical novelist holds a mirror up to the mirror. Except for the distance between the two mirrors, you would have a blank, a vacuum. The distance is everything. The two facing mirrors do not exclude life but include more of it than has been included before. Those Dutch painters who specialized in interiors very often put in a mirror in order to show the part of the room that was outside the picture frame. They also kept firmly in mind what was outside the limits of the picture or hidden by a wall or a curtain so firmly in mind that though you see through the open window only a very small view of a street or a garden, you know what the rest is like. If you see through a doorway into the next room, you know that room.

When the autobiographical writer does not have a didactic purpose, he has some other purposes, which you, the reader, are gradually aware of. He is trying to free himself from something that plagues him, such as an unhappy love. Or he has a secret that he must talk about and not talk about. Or he hates his father. Or he has committed a crime. Or perhaps the criminal impulse is unconscious and yet he blames himself for it as if it were something actually done. As a child he was angry with his mother about something— so angry that he wishes she were dead. She dies, of natural causes, and he blames himself as remorsefully as if he had held a pillow over her face, like poor Othello, until she stopped breathing. Very often, though not always, the autobiographical novelist is partly a poet, and feels an impulse to share with the poet not only his language but his subject matter. Or he has become, through experience, aware of a psychological truth that cannot be proved except in terms of his knowledge of his own self.

Also, he is an innovator. He wants to give a greater place in the technique of the novel to memory. He wants to give objects the status of characters. He wants to describe sensations not hitherto pinned down, the interplay of the senses. He wants to describe the double life that goes on in everyone of us between the past and the present. He wants to do the interest of the mind in its own self. This often dismaying, often boring, never-ending interior monologue can be bent on self-deception, but it can also be focused on a slow painful discovery of the truth. The autobiographical novelist is a kind of explorer, making his way through a country that is never going to be very well mapped, and therefore you have a choice between reading him and going through the experience yourself.

Private remarks.

Mostly on the subject of pure reminiscence versus autobiographical writing.

IN INFERIOR HANDS details lose their charm, the subjects, the scenes get one by one disposed of, the form is most often ultimately exasperating. A catalog. A collection of things such as are saved in the attic, the attic being in this case the mind.

What drives a person toward reminiscence is an unsolved problem which is in essence dramatic, and so the form becomes fused with the narrative form of the novel. The older writers would not have recognized it as such. Would have objected to the personal intrusions, the facts not sufficiently concealed, the weakness of invention.

But in the area of the autobiographical novel, every substitution is for the worse. A flaw. There are no correspondences, there is only the exact recording of a life, which derives its authority from the fact that this is what happened, and its meaning from what the narrator brings to it in the way of understanding and sensibility.

It can stand additions but not substitutions.

It opens up all sorts of personal moral problems. The writer is constantly with one foot over the line into libel and violation of personal privacy. He is dangerous to know. The good writer is never out to get some real person, but real people can suddenly find they have or have not been damaged.

Because the autobiographical writer is unsparing with himself he feels that this earns him the right to treat candidly of others. It is all a morass, unsolvable on the moral plane. It is better to assume that talent doesn't care where it resides and all writers are suffering from a defective moral sense, the result of an increased capacity in other areas, the imagination, the sense of order, the vision of human life. But keep away from them. They can be dangerous.

Remarks on writing, written, so far as I can tell, in Maxwell's forties.

IN ANY KIND of professional writing, it is important to decide where your ambition lies, which star your wagon is to be hitched to, and then very carefully in the beginning, less carefully later keep tabs on what subjects are being published and disposed of. The older an author is, the less important his subject matter, the more important what he himself brings to it. Usually a young writer is not sufficiently crystallized as a personality and so what he brings to his subject is not enough to justify a retreatment of a recently or already familiar theme.

The dependence on actuality. The truth has at least always significance. Fiction does too, but on a different level, often disguised from the person inventing it, because it serves a psychological purpose, whereas a series of actual events show choice in operation, cause and effect, all manner of things from which the psychological purpose working backward can be deduced.

Unless you are very lucky, the drama of an actual series of events is liable to go inward rather than outward, to such an extent that it upsets the instinctive requirement of the reader that something happen. Interiorly, all is change, everything happens over and over to such an extent that nothing new happens, and there is a feeling that some step forward must be involved, the characters different, or their situation at least different at the end than at the beginning.

None of this holds as an absolute generalization. Making rules is a mental exercise.

If there is not in you somewhere an innate storyteller, you are not a novelist, and the effect of what you write will determine this. If an editor or reader says I don't care what happens to these people, it is a warning. If too many people say the same thing, you can be fairly certain that you are not a storyteller, because the storyteller originally worked for his living, and this meant holding his audience, or no cash.

But it is also possible that a storyteller is not allowed to function freely, because of considerations that have nothing to do with art. Personal responsibilities, moral feelings, psychological fears, lack of courage, lack of interest in the truth. This is most true of the autobiographical novel, which is much more common now than formerly, though it always had its place. Jane Austen was autobiographical, Fannie Burney watched carefully what went on in her father's house, and the quality that makes them seem objective is their ability to disguise actuality, retaining the essence while freely shifting the details and outward form.

The importance of writing in an ivory tower. The misapprehension derives from the ivory, not the tower, which suggests that the author turn his back on life, whereas he does just the opposite, he looks directly at it, but from a height, offered only by climbing a flight, or several flights of stairs.

My first novel was written literally in a tower—a water tank on a Wisconsin farm, three flights up, where, when invention flagged I could go out on a little platform among the treetops and check up on what was going on around me. Sometimes I had to descend and walk around before I could find what I was after, but then I went back up into the tower, and this constituted an act of detachment, nothing from below could interfere with the idea that I had just taken up with me. You must be involved only as far as it is useful to be involved. There has to be some protective door that can be closed on the continuously changing world, so that the bombardment of personality is controlled, and held in check. The imaginary actions are more real to you than any actual ones.

Even if your characters are taken from life and are within calling distance, you are not dependent on them, on what they will do next, because the key to what they will do next is in you as well as in them. You will find yourself anticipating their remarks and their actions in a sometimes uncanny way.

If they are not taken immediately from life around you, then there is all the more reason to detach yourself from your situation and attach yourself to another closer one—whether in memory or in imagination or in a single fructifying experience.

A critic is a help, and the care with which you choose your critic will determine his usefulness. He should know, actually or instinctively, the material you are writing about. He should know you. That is, know when you were writing as yourself and when you are under outside influences, and not yourself. And you yourself must ultimately submit to this criticism and rise above it. As you submit to your own criticism and rise above it.

The influence on Flaubert of Alfred le Poitevin and Louis Bouilhet, one of whom had no talent whatsoever, and the other was only a minor one, but he was able to direct Flaubert into a realm, against Flaubert's will, where his talent flourished.

The critic need not be a professional writer, critic or editor. Their judgment is also helpful after you are through, but only in a limited way. It will tell you what you have accomplished, but rather too late to do anything about this book, and of more value for the book that you write next. In any case you have once more to submit to it and rise above it, before it will be a value.

Don't hold back on the first or in fact on any novel. The material, the themes, will many of them be used again, but not in the same way, because you will not be the same person. And everything you have is never more than just enough for the purpose at hand.

You need not fear very much that a genuine talent will not be appreciated by editors and reviewers, of the present day. They are on the whole perceptive enough of new talent, and where they are lacking is perhaps a sustaining interest, in the continuous work of writers. Their pleasure in the discovery of new talent interferes somewhat with their ability to keep track of their old discoveries, and having once perceived the existence of talent they have a tendency to wash their hands of it. Which is perhaps all to the good. It forces back upon the author the responsibility for making his audience, each time, and if necessary, as his work changes, making a new audience that will respond to it.

In the writing of novels there are two activities that run concurrently—the recreation of life as the author sees it, and a judgment upon the characters and the scenes that he has conceived. To re-create life all that is necessary is to have lived it. To judge it, requires that one have observed more than those aspects and relationships that touch one's own life. This requires a little time. The first three years out of college is not too long to postpone the beginning of a novel. During the postponement, it helps to do anything that sharpens judgment, reading, reviewing, teaching anything that focuses the attention outside one's own work.

The literary judgment can be precociously developed, and not be either dependable or sustaining. This is usually the result of too much reading of other people's judgment, and not the exercise of judgment oneself.

Experience is necessary, but unavoidable. The cliché of the author who has been a dishwasher, etc.

You have, in your hands, a novel when you are aware, either from observation or personal experience, of a fairly complicated series of events that have come to some kind of conclusion, so that anything further would be merely repetitious, and not change or explain the nature of what really happened. Possibly this is too self-conscious. Possibly by the time it occurs to you that any subject would be interesting as the subject of a novel, it is already finished, unconsciously, for the time being.

Taking notes on conduct instead of relying on the unconscious mind to sift what is valuable and retain it.

When I was beginning to write I saw the short story as being a kind of safe with a combination. They tended to be about a single situation, a single moment, in a single place. You arrived at the combination and the door of the safe swung open, revealing a short (very short, ten pages maybe) story. This kind of story was, I think, a swing of the pendulum away from the kind of story that embraces the whole of life.

Fragment concerning *The Folded Leaf,* written for an occasion but unpublished.

THERE ARE AS many different ways of writing a novel probably as there are novels. In that beautiful book of reminiscences, *Three Worlds,* Carl van Vechten tells how Elinor Wylie "began a sentence on her typewriter only when it was finished in her mind and needed no corrections. In the entire manuscript of *The Venetian Glass Nephew* there was hardly a change even of a syllable, to the page." Whenever I have an occasion to go to the attic I see there, in a box, a pile of manuscript fourteen inches high. It consists of the first, second, and third versions of "The Folded Leaf," together with certain stray chapters, unfinished incidents, outlines written down in what seemed like the heat of inspiration and never looked at again. The pile would be higher if a good many pages had not found their way directly into the fireplace.

The labor of polishing and rewriting accounts for most of this pile of manuscript, but I never look at it without realizing that, buried there, are scenes that deserved a better fate: The night Lymie Peters spent in an Indian pueblo, and what happened when he went to solemn high mass at the Church of the Advent in Boston. Also that automobile accident on a mountain road outside of Albuquerque, and the conversation in a park in Hartford, Connecticut, a conversation about love between Lymie and a girl who continued to be devoted to Spud Latham after he had grown tired of her. About abandoned characters I feel even more guilt. Lymie Peters' stepmother, for example, who tried so hard to teach him to pick up his clothes, and the college boy who used to weep with frustration because he couldn't understand Immanuel Kant, and that other friend of Lymie's, the boy whose childhood had been spent happily in the Philippine Islands and who very nearly managed to live, in a middlewestern University, the life of an aborigine.

So far as I can see now, there is nothing wrong with these rejected characters, no reason why these unpublished scenes would not read as well as any that appear in the final version. I never of my own free will rejected them. They were rejected by the characters of the novel, who, at a certain point in the writing of the fourth version, took over, spoke with their own voices, determined their own actions, and decided at last the pattern that the novel would follow. This is, I suspect, the common experience of most novelists. The only odd thing is that none of this written material can ever be used in any other way. It owes its existence to the story that it was once a part of; and the fact that, in the final shaping of this story, these scenes and characters were discovered to be irrelevant, doesn't in any way free them from it. In the attic they will remain.

About a final version, once it is published, there is very little that any author can or now cares to say. "The Folded Leaf" is done as well as I knew how to do it at the time. If I were to write a fifth version it would be somewhat different. For one thing, I would try to explain Mr. Peters, who deserves more sympathy and understanding than I gave him, and I could improve on the ending. If I wrote a sixth version five years from now, it would again be different from the version I might do now. "The Folded Leaf" is that kind of a novel. The whole book might be written in the manner and style of the lyrical asides . . .

Writing about adolescents, from a journal.

ANY NOVELIST WRITING seriously about adolescents finds himself faced with a continual obligation to justify his choice of material. In writing about grown people, you assume that if you write honestly the reader will be interested, identify himself perhaps with one of the characters, and follow along to any conclusions you are able to arrive at. If you write about children, you can safely draw on the reader's desire to relive his own childhood. But if you write about adolescents, the question that immediately arises is how to make them seem important enough to read about. This is partly due to the literary tradition of Thomas Bailey Aldrich and Booth Tarkington, which presents growing up as something inescapably comic; and partly due to certain facts of our culture. Adolescents are allowed no part in the political life of the nation. If they find a job this does not, as with grown people, confer economic independence upon them. They are encouraged to study and to play football, but not to marry or to find any direct release from sexual tension. For what is, anthropologically speaking, an unreasonably long time they are forced to take a passive part in the life around them.

The question arises of how to give them meaning in the world, a world in which, in our culture, they play a very slight part. They cannot vote, few of them marry, most of their activity is circumscribed by the schoolroom and by the fact that even though their hearts are broken, they have to be in bed by nine o'clock.

It is generally assumed that all adolescents are immature, as if maturity were conferred automatically on a man or woman the moment they are old enough to vote. Actually, maturity is conferred on no one and few attain it this side of the grave. The important thing about adolescents is not that they are immature, but that they are forced to take a passive part, to wait, their talents unused, and for the most part undiscovered, their destiny as much as a matter of mystery to them as if they had not yet been born, with no life open to them except the life of feeling. That this is the richest most complex life of all, nobody ever tells them, and they have no way of judging for themselves. You can have your heart broken at fifteen as easily as at any other age, and the fact that you have to be home at nine o'clock on school nights adds indignity to tragedy.

Their conversation, if overheard, is nearly always trivial or foolish or dull, because they have not yet learned that it is possible to talk about the things that really interest them and be understood. But actually, what they are engaged in, the process of growing up, is both serious and important, as serious and important as any experience except death, and something like it.

Remarks delivered to accept awards.

Speech accepting the Brandeis Creative Arts Award and Medal, in 1984, an occasion on which the writer Paula Fox was also honored.

A YOUNG FRENCHWOMAN once informed me that there is only one way to say thank you in French; gradations of gratitude have to be conveyed by other means than words. This medal is a very real reassurance to me, both because of what it means and because of the distinction of the committee that conferred it.

There is no right or wrong way to approach the writing of prose fiction, Henry James to the contrary. It works if it has the breath of life in it, and if not not. I spent yesterday afternoon reading Paula Fox's *The Western Coast* and the characters she brought into being with such a light touch were so vivid to me that I could not sleep last night for thinking about them. I want to say thank you to her also.

Mostly what I have wanted to do in fiction was to defend what I remember. The fate that any individual creature and most things can expect is oblivion. To go against this is, if you take the long view, simply perverse. But I find it emotionally unacceptable even so. And have tried, in a small way, to circumvent it. Enumeration of persons, places, and events is, of course, not enough. There has to be a loving rearrangement so that the experience can exist independently of the experiencer, who can then stand back from what he has done and be moved by it.

Life being so terribly short, and without guarantees against disaster, it is something that by picking up a book what we know to be true we can place in the widest possible context, and take the world in through eyes and hearts that are not our own. We have this always accessible form of reincarnation. Before my daughters had mastered the alphabet they used to climb into my lap and say, "Read, read." The divine hunger.

> Speech on receiving the Gold Medal for Fiction from the American Academy of Arts and Letters in 1995. On the day of the ceremony, Maxwell had expected to be in Europe, on a trip that he and his wife had planned for some time, but they didn't go, and he read the speech himself, in fact he recited it, having committed it to memory. This is the version he had given me to deliver in his stead. Except for the line that is crossed out, it is the one he gave.

WHEN I WAS a little boy, among my worries was the house I was born in. It wasn't as nice as the house we were by that time living in and it didn't look very substantial to me, and I was afraid it would no longer be there when the time came for them to put up the plaque.

Over the years my expectations have moderated. I discovered that where I belonged, and where I wanted to be, was not in the White House but with the story-tellers.

~~All power corrupts, but storytelling moves the mind and broadens the heart and breeds understanding.~~

I rejoice in this honor, which I did not expect, and which it comes as somewhat but not entirely a surprise that I could be thought to deserve.

I wish I had written *The Great Gatsby*. I wish I had written *In the Ravine* and *Ward Number 6*. I wish I had written *The House in Paris*. I wish I had written *The Sportsman's Notebook*. But the novelist has to work with what life has given him. It was no small gift that I grew up in a small town in the Middle West where the elm trees cast a pattern of light and shade over the pavement, and also that my father and mother loved each other, since it turned out that love was the subject that interested me more than any other.

Speech delivered in 1998 on the occasion of a dinner at the Century Association to honor Maxwell's fifty years of membership.

LOOKING BACK OVER my shoulder I see, beginning with my twenty-eighth year when I went to work for *The New Yorker*, such an unbroken line of good fortune that it doesn't seem possible it all happened to one person. The lonely bachelor found himself with a family to cherish, and I was able to earn a living in a way that was congenial to me. In the beginning I was asked now and then to take a sow's ear and make it read like a silk purse but during my later years as an editor I had only gifted writers whose work I delighted in and who mostly became dear friends.

If I had continued to be an editor five days a week I would undoubtedly have stopped writing. But my luck held and I ended up working three days a week at the office and the remaining four at home, in my bathrobe and slippers, writing. Some writers have said that writing was agony to them but I love making sentences and toward the end of a given piece of work am likely to become euphoric and too easily pleased. I would then take what seemed a finished piece of work to the critic on the hearth, who would read it carefully and then say, "I think this is going to be very good," and send me back to my typewriter for the final necessary effort. When she was satisfied, I knew I had done it and had nothing to worry about.

In the end the stories and novels that wanted to be written got written and Judith Jones and the publishing firm of Alfred Knopf didn't bat an eye when I presented them with book after book that we knew wasn't likely to sell more than forty-five hundred copies. And my daughter Brookie designed dust jackets for many of them that are a satisfaction to me every time I see them. And my daughter Kate is no mean proof reader.

A year ago I came down with pneumonia and I have been told I nearly didn't make it, but I did make it, and I'm here, at this party, and can say, "Bless you for coming."

At ninety I am beyond any serious literary effort but I did want to mark this occasion with some sentences written with pleasure.

In the late nineteen-forties Eugene Saxton, my editor at Harper and Brothers, took me to lunch at the Century a number of times and on one of those occasions he asked me if I would like him to propose me for membership in the Club. While I was waiting for my name to come up before the Admissions Committee, my wife's uncle, Reinold Noyes, gave a lunch for me and invited half a dozen Centurions that he hoped might put their names in the candidate book. Among them were two men—Rodman Gilder and Austin Strong—who, when I became a member went out of their way to make me feel comfortable and happy in these handsome surroundings. They were more than twenty years older than I was and had been friends since their youth and what it felt like was that their friendship had simply opened to include me. As a kind of mascot. When I walked into the club at 12:30 my eyes would be searching for them. Often I found them together. Austin Strong was a playwright, Rodman Gilder a literary journalist.

His father, Richard Watson Gilder, was the editor of *Scribner's Monthly*, which became *The Century Illustrated Monthly Magazine*, a periodical of importance during the last quarter of the nineteenth century. Rodman's mother, Helena de Kay, was a painter and according to the Columbia Encyclopedia her home was a literary and artistic center. It did not appear to weigh on Rodman that he was the son of so famous a man and the son-in-law of an even more famous one, the designer Louis Tiffany.

Rodman was sensible, humorous and candid. He was also a very handsome man. I remarked once that he looked

Spanish and he said, "It could well be. What was left of the Spanish Armada was smashed to pieces on the West Coast of Ireland, where my ancestors came from." He made no effort to appear witty but I noticed that after he had hit the nail on the head he didn't go on hammering at it. In my grandfather's library there was a decade or so of the bound volumes of the *Century Magazine*, which as a boy I used to read on rainy days, and it delighted Rodman when I would sometimes come up with the name of some novelist or illustrator whose reputation had long since faded from the common memory. His most substantial work, "The Battery," is about four centuries of the events, often bizarre, that took place at the southern tip of Manhattan.

Recently a note from him fell out of a book and it is very like his conversation. "The fortnightly dinners are 'optional' as to uniform. So by all means come (1) disguised as a dentist (as the French say); or (2) in white tie as a Reinold of the Old School; or in ordinary black tie; or in beret and horizontally striped jersey; or in Centurion Hoover double-breasted blue; or in Don Adams tweeds; or in commuter's clothes flecked with egg. The main thing is to arrive."

His manner with Austin Strong was gently teasing. Smiling across the table at him he said to me, "As a young playwright Austin was extremely prolific. He used to ring the doorbell of our house in Washington Square along about ten o'clock. Just when mother and father were thinking of going up to bed. They knew it was him, and they used to hope that it was a one act and not a three act play that he wanted them to listen to."

Austin's most successful play, "Seventh Heaven," had been made into an even more successful movie, with Janet Gaynor and Charles Farrell. It was about love in a garret. The hero was blinded in the first World War, and it could be counted on to reduce a considerable part of the audience to tears. One day, sitting next to him at the long table, I spoke of it and he began to talk about other plays of his that he thought better of but that had never been produced. One of them was set in the alimentary canal, and he took an envelope from his inside coat pocket and on it drew the scenery for me. We lingered talking until we were the only ones at the table. Messages and phone calls accumulated on my desk at *The New Yorker*. The waiters cleared the table and reset them. We went on talking, till four o'clock in the afternoon.

Sitting in a winged chair at the magazine table, he told me that his grandmother married Robert Louis Stevenson and that he had passed a good part of his boyhood in Stevenson's house in Samoa and was engaged in writing a series of pieces about it for the *Atlantic Monthly*. It wasn't hard to get him to talk about Stevenson; what was hard was to enjoy his undivided attention. Friends of his would cross the room to speak to him and I would have to wait until some other day for the end of the story.

I have since discovered the group photograph—it is in most Stevenson biographies—of the household at Vailima, standing or seated on the lower veranda: RLS (in a rumpled white shirt and trousers) and Fanny Stevenson (with her chin resting in her hand and looking like a world famous author); Stevenson's mother, in her widow's weeds, and next to her the maid she brought with her from Scotland; Lloyd Osborne, Fanny's son by her first husband; Joe Strong, Austin's father, in a sarong with a parrot on his shoulder; the Samoan house steward, cook, assistant cook (cradling an axe), cattleman, plantation hand, and cattle boy—strapping men in *lava lavas*, looking more like warriors (which they sometimes were), than domestic servants. Austin, a bare-legged little boy in shorts and a striped blazer, is sitting on the steps and leaning against his mother, Belle Strong. She was a beautiful, admirable, intelligent woman. During the final years of Stevenson's life he suffered from writer's cramp and he dictated not only his narrative writing but his correspondence to her. Sometimes when she felt he was straying from the truth in a letter she would insert a parenthetical correction. It says something about their relationship that he allowed her to do this.

Austin never spoke about his father, who was a successful portrait painter until excessive conviviality turned him into an habitual drunkard. Fanny Stephenson once described him as "a sweet, engaging, aggravating creature, refined, artistic, affectionate, and weak as water, living in vague dreams. One needs to be a millionaire to support him and a philosopher to love him." Austin's mother got a divorce from him and he married a native woman and went right on making trouble.

I am not sure what good it does to describe the physical appearance of someone when it is their nature that you were mostly aware of when you were talking to them and that is the basis for the attachment, but anyway he was of ordinary height, with a broad head, a dusky red-dish complexion, and a smile that would warm the heart of a cannibal. Must have, since they came and went at Vailima and were sometimes even employed there. His voice was unhurried and his eyes saw you. I sensed that he could be angry and impatient, but never experienced either in him. Only infinite kindness. The islands had left their mark on him. He was at ease in his own body and would not have looked silly with a hibiscus blossom tucked behind his ear.

I saw them away from the club only on two occasions. He and his very beautiful wife spent their summers in an 18th-century red-brick house on the main street of Nan-tucket. I paid a call on him there once and we sat on a little porch overlooking the harbor. He talked about the pleasures he had year after year teaching adolescent boys and girls to sail.

The following winter when he did not appear at the Club for a week or so I inquired of the doorman about him and was told that he had been unwell but was better and that Mrs. Strong had said visitors would be welcome. I went looking for Rodman, who said soberly, "Heart attack." When I was led upstairs to Austin's bedroom I found him sitting up in a four poster. Except for his poor color he was his usual self. He said he would be back in the club soon. Instead I found myself attending his funeral. Shortly after that, Rodman sat back in his chair, with one arm behind his head to think about something, and never finished the thought. That made two funerals. I said, I will never again love an old man. They die on you.

For many years the memorials in the Century Year-book were written by the archivist, George W. Martin. They were simple and straightforward and not sicklied o'er with the pale cast of propriety. If a deceased member had been rather too fond of the bottle, the archivist said so—not in a censorious way but as if it was the cross the poor man had to bear. I enjoyed reading the memorials even of people I didn't know, because they were real lives, not official ones. I don't know whether it was me or chance that Rodman Gilder's name was never mentioned in my hearing or whether the Century is a kind of Never Never Land and the unbearable can't get past the heavy front door. But in any case I didn't know that before I met Rodman, the worst that could happen to him had happened. "He had a son," the archivist said. "Richard Watson Gilder, who was elected to the Century in 1942. The boy went off to the War, and, alas, was lost with his plane. After the War there was a ceremony held in the club in honor of the members *morts pour la patrie*. Rodman came of course. A tender affectionate citation of the boy was read by Bishop Aldrich, while all the members stood up. At the end, when the staff sang the Battle Hymn of the Republic from the Upper Hall, the tears coursed down poor Rodman's cheeks. The Lord bless and keep him."

Austin's memorial struck me as accurate but slightly askew. I am quoting: "Austin was at the Club a great deal, pleasantly and happily occupied there. He had an understanding heart, and was loyal and incautious and wholly without guile. He never compromised with the truth as he saw it, for the sake of expediency, and so he bound his friends to him with hoops of steel." But was the archivist saying that Austin wasn't everybody's cup of tea? Talking about him once with a woman who had an antique shop on Nantucket and knew Austin much better than I did, I remarked that so many people were drawn to him that it must at times have been a problem to him, and she said, "No. He chose the people he charmed."

Eventually I remembered the pieces he had said he was doing for the *Atlantic Monthly* and I went to the periodical guide at the Society Library to find out what issues they were in. There was nothing. Either they had never reached a publishable state or they had existed only in his head. There were two listings in *Reader's Digest*. One of them turned out to be how, as a small boy, he caught and carried off in his hat a very rare two tailed ornamental goldfish belonging to his Oceanic Majesty King Kalakaua of the Hawaiian Archipelago. Who was, fortunately, acquainted with Austin's father and mother. The other was a Most Unforgettable Character I Have Ever Known piece—not, to my surprise, about RLS but about Fanny Stevenson, seen somewhat through rose colored glasses. However it contains an interesting account of the Strongs' voyage from San Francisco to Honolulu. Austin was still an infant. They couldn't afford the Pacific liner but sailed instead on a small trading schooner, in very rough weather. The lee rail was often under a wash of green water. One of the sailors tied a double bowline around Austin's waist and made the other end of the rope fast to a ring bolt, to keep him from being washed overboard.

Of the stories he told me I remember only this one, perhaps because I found it so affecting. There was no school on the island that Austin could be sent to and his schooling at home was sketchy. Every morning at ten Stevenson interrupted his writing and taught Austin history—Scottish history, the only history that Stevenson knew. Old Mrs. Stevenson set him to memorizing poetry. "'To a Skylark.' Byron. Scott. 'The Splendor falls on castle walls.'" And his mother dealt with arithmetic and other subjects.

When Stevenson died, the women decided that the time had come for Austin to have a proper education and they enrolled him in school in New Zealand that was more English ever than a boys' school in England would have been.

"My mother could not buy clothes for me in Samoa," he said. "She took me to a German tailor in Apia, who cut down a man's suit for me. When I arrived at the school the boys looked at me and decided I was the funniest thing they had ever seen. They rolled on the ground with laughter. And it didn't end there. It went on day after day. I didn't know how to make them stop laughing at me. Or even how to talk to them. The only conversation I had ever heard was the conversation at the dinner table of highly intelligent adults. I was so homesick that I thought I would die of it. Until the day of the swimming matches. The other boys had been taught to swim like proper English boys. I had been taught to swim by the natives. I won all the races. When I came out of the water after the last one, the Lord Chief Justice was standing on the shore and he wrapped his robes around me . . . ."

I have often wondered why the Lord Chief Justice of New Zealand was wearing his robes at this sporting event, but in any case he wrapped them around the wet child and took him home with him and taught him how to set a boys' school on its ear.

Notes for stories.

FIVE PEOPLE, ALL waiting on the same day, in different places, to be given the same honor, which only one can have. The differences between their hopes and their reasonable expectation. How they react toward hope. Holding it at arm's length or just feeling it or saying they don't care. Dealing with disappointment in advance, confident that they will get the honor, assuring other people and themselves that they won't get it. Watching first the calendar and then not watching the clock. Pleased that they have an engagement and at the same time imagining the phone call that will come just before they go to the engagement. See the note left by the maid on the hall table, to call so-and-so, who would only be calling about that. Realizing that now they can let go, it has happened, and it didn't happen to them. Making decisions about how they will act when they get what at the very same instant they are telling themselves they will not get. The hour of the meeting of the committee occurring to them again and again, a vision of the beginning, of the judge's lack of sympathy, as, in the same instance, they write an imaginary thank you letter to one of the judges for being the one who must've been responsible for their getting the honor.

One a recluse who may reject it.

One a woman so far gone in folie de grandeur that she confidently expects it.

One young and counting on his luck, with good reason.

One innocent and simply happy in a childish way.

One bitter, resentful, and at the same time hopeful. Balancing a lifetime of neglect (not quite true) with the fact that the honor is no longer as important as it once was, and will make no difference in his situation. Should be the person who gets it.

I sometimes think that other people know everything; that we never deceive anyone but ourselves.

George Scott looked at his wife over the top of the newspaper. The children had to be told constantly not to rock and teeter in their chairs, and she had spoken in an ordinary tone of voice, so why did he look at her that way? As a country man looks at the sky for information about the weather? The question, whatever it was, remained unanswered. One would think that the longer people have been married, the fewer the secrets they are keeping from each other, but it is unfortunately the opposite in most cases . . .

Standing in front of the bathroom mirror, with a razor in his right hand and his face lathered with shaving soap, George Scott came to a solemn conclusion: there was a fatal flaw in his character: nobody was ever as real to him as his own self.

From "Over by the River":
"With his safety razor ready to begin a downward sweep, George Carrington studied the lathered face in the mirror of the medicine cabinet. He shook his head. There was a fatal flaw in his character. Nobody was ever as real to him as he was to himself. If people knew how little he cared whether they lived or died, they wouldn't want to have anything to do with him."

An elderly woman calling a young couple on the phone and asking them to cocktails, and enjoying the sounds of life that come over the phone, the banging, and children's voices—after the quiet that settled down on her so many years ago.

Describe a lineup of taxis, and send them off, one by one, and then follow them. In which case the novel would be called The Taxi Stand. But this has no possibilities of development.

A man, for no reason, decides to (no reason but his age) to pick up the lapsed threads of his life. Or he's bothered because they have lapsed, and his past and his present have no connection, and his past and the life of his family none either. He spent an evening with old friends, shares in their enthusiasm, and has the feeling that he *has* achieved something, but they are only passing through town. The pile of unanswered letters, from Christmas—for he hasn't entirely lost connection. And then the first discovery, the people he loved ambivalently did not love him at all.

He thinks of writing to his best friend in his youth, and is afraid to, remembers what the friend was really like and decides that it isn't safe. He begins to doubt the truth of his own memories, and then finds that he doesn't trust other people's memories either. Nevertheless, he absents himself from conversations in order to relive brilliant moments in the past. His daydreams take the form not of what would he would like but of what happened. Now the past is so much with him, it is only his idea of the past, a dream.

The constant pattern of dreaming is the continual contact with the past.

A scene: the French lessons at the Berlitz. They air their grievances in French, and the teacher is confronted with an argument between married people, who are more frank in front of a third person and in another language.

A man who imagines hostility and enemies, not insane, but carefully and reasonably put together evidence, and then finds that they are not true, and then, helplessly, finds a new hostility somewhere else and begins to fit the pieces of that pattern together. All depends on the details, involving money, acts of kindness that were not necessary, etc. and finally, catching himself at it, stops in his tracks, helpless and frightened, not knowing who is friend and who is enemy, or whether he is trembling on the brink of going insane. The sky, the details of life all around him are reassuring and he proves to himself that he is not mentally unstable, but then it begins again, half an idea which he brushes out of his mind, like a gnat. This is a story, all right. It just needs writing and details. It also requires a complete character who cannot be used again, with a life, a family, a home, a job, everything. But it is worth doing.

> Maxwell worked on *The Chateau* for something like sixteen years. During that time, the writer Frank O'Connor and his wife, Harriet Sheehy, came to lunch at the Maxwells' house in the country. Maxwell talked about the book, which seemed shapeless and only getting longer, and O'Connor offered to read it. He left with two cardboard boxes of pages. He read them and said that he thought there were two books in them, one a travel book about France and the other a novel about two Americans, a husband and wife, making a tour of France. Maxwell thought that if there were two books he could surely make one from them. Before this, though, he wrote:

WHAT IS MISSING at this point is an understood relevance, an arrangement toward an end that is also understood, and so offers a principle of rejection. The story is in serious danger, like life, of descending into commonplaces, which are disconnected and lead toward no illumination whatever. There are three main characters, not yet established, one of them not even foreshadowed, and strong minor characters with no relevance as yet, and a dozen minor characters to be put to some or no use, depending on my resourcefulness. What is going to happen? This, instead of being a story about explosions, espionage, and murder, is concerned with nothing more fatal than hurt feelings. How to make them worthy of investigation, as they must be, because they are feelings. First of all the people must be capable of feeling, and second they must be hostile toward other people, or they wouldn't imagine and create hostility in others. This hostility must be unconscious. Madame Judel's is conscious, open aggression, and she probably never is hurt. The Americans must be changed, must in some way be affected by their experience with the French people, and so must the French people be affected by knowing the Americans. But the theme ought to be announced. Not clearly, but in such a way that the reader, looking back, will remember and say, why it was all there, in that one paragraph toward the beginning. Also, the element of choice must be involved, or there is no drama, and so far there has been no occasion for choosing. It is as yet too much a record of our actual travel. Not a story. At the point when the Americans enter the house, the house must enter into them.

If you cannot invent, record.

Another story idea.

THE OLD MAN with the young wife, wanting to rest, and his sister's anger at what is being done to him, his efforts mocked, met with impatience. What at first seems to keep him from growing old is in the end the hastener of his death, which is what his wife wants, since she is tired herself of marriage and wants a period of freedom. She feels, through him, the approach of old age, and wants to crowd as much in before she herself becomes inactive, in poor health. In the beginning years of their marriage she became older, to be with him, now she drags him back to her age, without mercy, but after his death she will have no mercy for herself.

An exercise of free association.

PILLOW SWORD WORD sward lawnmower fixed holes of mice or moles roller Holy roller Bank roll, Martiniquan taxi driver Bill Driver works in bank tank where the wild flowers grow up the rushes O this England Mitchesan Sparta, Ruth and Naomi, amid the alien corn bad writing poetry of the experimental twenties, $20 bills at bank window . . . . I feel tired, want to sink down and sleep, weep. Blame, in shame. This beginning time of energy this spring, I feel the call to action, and no energy, exhausted by the demands of winter. Winter take all. Hall, ball, bawl my eyes out, Oedipus, club foot, foot the bill, Bill take a dose of epsom salts . . . today is the day they give babies away. hands, Sister Mary Alice rejecting my hands as too small to play the piano. soft you now the fair Ophelia. Roses, bumpus, tits, two bits, bit in your teeth. Where in the past am I . . . Show me the way to go home. I am tired and I want to lay down by the River Jordan. almonds, alms, almoner, quivering shimmering weakness behind the eyelids . . . the taste of my coffee tired me. Shall the salt lose its savor. Where is my joy, my boy, beamish, Miss Beam in your own eye. for an eye and a tooth for truth. ruth with rue my heart is laden, come unto me, all ye weary and heavy laden . . . Ship, slip, gonorrhea, goneral. Beget a black child on a white sea, foam, home gloaming and my Bonnie by my side, Roman law, with your old heehawshkwaw, two visored cap, Hap, slap, rap, map of Europe, where we can't go . . . shirk, shirt, dirt, firk, jerk, lurk, Turk, murk berserk, Kirk . . . dovetail, lovetail, sale, hail hale and farewell, I hear the bell that summons me to heaven or to hell . . . country mouse and city mouse in her lousy playhouse, souse, douse, cold, shower bower flower . . . Are you tired, mired. Are you hired, fired. Are you washed in the blood of the lamb, I am. Sam hadgy-widgy ky-me-owe a wooding go. Slow. Row row row your boat, shoat, Ted in bed, dead, a hole in his head, a foal in the shed, painted red, instead of blue, show the mare and show it where the glare of hair dares to care. Wear a bright tie, deny the Lord's sword, the fear of the draft, of war in the world . . . smother another day.

The time of funerals.

The breaking of threads with the last of the older generation, so that all secrets will go with them.

Notes for "The Front and Back Parts of the House," published in *The New Yorker* in 1991 and in *Billie Dyer and Other Stories.* The story is about a visit Maxwell made to Lincoln when he was in his forties and his encounter with a woman named Hattie Dyer who worked for his mother as a maid and was now working for his aunt. Maxwell remembered her fondly, and without thinking, he put his arms around her, but she simply stood still. Her unresponsiveness led him to wonder if the past had really been the way he imagined it. He wrote a version of the story but had no real ending, because he didn't know why Dyer had rebuffed him. A few years later he got a letter from a cousin in Lincoln telling him that a Black man who did yard work for him was reading one of Maxwell's books, "And in a flash I realized what the unforgivable thing was and who had done it," he wrote. The explanation became the story's ending, which I don't think I should give away.

These notes are for the original version.

A mistake
neither did or said anything to
did nothing and said nothing to make it easier for me

to get from the kitchen back into the front part of the house where I belonged.

The terrain of Lincoln, the 9th Street hill, my hurry to try out the new bicycle, out of control, nothing on earth could stop it, fatalistically I prepared myself for whatever was going to happen and ended up with a skinned knee and a hole in my long black stocking.

The houses on 9th Street, on Elm Street, forming the top of the letter T, three or four small houses, all lived in by poor people, and in one of them lived the Dyers.

Mrs. Dyer the child of a slave, Hattie the first maid I can remember, she left to go to Chicago, and her daughter, left behind, was unsatisfactory, the dishes greasy. My mother got a white girl.

The man who put himself through medical school, to everyone's amusement. The history of the celebration of the hundredth anniversary of the town's founding, he was one of the ten distinguished men

My mother's death, the house sold, moving away, my aunt remained in the same house where she had always lived. When I went there with my wife and children, she said, I have a surprise for you. Dyer and the furnace. Mrs. Dyer and the laundry basket full of washing. My father's visits, to Mrs. Dyer, with the ten dollar bill.

I grew up thinking that there was an indissoluble attachment between our family and them. THE SUR-PRISE. It was no different from putting my arms around a wooden post. There was no more response than if I had put my arms around

She did not even look at me

The book of theater programs

my mother and the family who wanted to move in across the street

She may not have been fond of my mother

Because my mother was fond of her, didn't mean she was fond of my mother. Or perhaps, it was such a long time ago, she neither remembered nor cared what my mother had been like. In Chicago she had had a different life, full of God knows what amount of trouble. The fact that she had once worked in a house where there was a little boy and I was that little boy was in any case a matter of indifference to her. She neither said nor did anything. My mother's death was a tragedy to me but not to her. She had other tragedies in all probability that I would never know about.

Working methods.

From a letter Maxwell wrote me, dated Halloween, 1989.

IN READING THE books that are written about in *The Outermost Dream* I used to mark the passages I liked as I read, and then when I had finished, go back and see what they consisted of. And wish a review could be made up of nothing but quotations from the book. But since it couldn't, I would try to find a way to connect them in a rational fashion. I never think of myself as thinking, but only of concentrating on some intention. And thinking to myself, there is a word, I know there is a word that would say exactly what I feel or mean, and being happy when I manage to find it.* I don't think you can be a writer at all and not take delight in what other writers do.

_____
* The way you feel when you decide on the right necktie.

Two quotations pinned to the bulletin board above Maxwell's desk:

"TOWARD THE END of his life Frank O'Connor described his idea of what a short story should be: 'It's about a moment of change in a person's life. It's a bright light falling on an action in such a way that the landscape of that person's life assumes a new shape. Something happens—the iron is bent—and anything that happens to that person afterwards, they never feel the same about again.'"

From an obituary in the *New York Times* for the singer Judith Raskin, a lyric soprano, and a family friend whom Kate Maxwell studied with.

"I'VE TRIED TO make up in depth what I don't have in quantity. There is a kind of singer who has a poetic approach to music rather than a purely vocal approach. It's a special kind of voice, which cannot be described simply as lyric or lyric coloratura. It's a special kind of sound with a certain purity, and I like to think that's what I have."

PART III

CRITICISM, TRIBUTES, MEMORIALS

Stevenson Revealed

> Maxwell wrote about Robert Louis Stevenson on four occasions, all of them for *The New Yorker*. Three pieces are published in *The Outermost Dream*. This is the fourth, from 1994.

Robert Louis Stevenson was forty-four when he was felled by a cerebral hemorrhage and never regained consciousness. He died on December 3, 1894.

Centennials are irresistible. Stevenson's house in Samoa, which was severely damaged by hurricanes and restored from the foundations, has been opened to the public for the first time. The Drambuie Edinburgh Film Festival devoted a weekend to his influence on cinema. Original manuscripts, photographs, and first editions have been on display at the National Library of Scotland and the Beinecke Library at Yale, where there was also an international symposium. Groups of people are going to follow the route Stevenson took with his unobliging donkey in the mountains of the Cévennes, and others, in Edinburgh, have looked at slides showing the flight, in *Kidnapped*, of Alan Breck and David Balfour through the Scottish Highlands. The Old Monterey Preservation Society offered a Silverado Tour, and twenty writers are convening at Fontainebleau—to do what, I don't know. Talk, probably.

At the time of Stevenson's death, there was no more widely read or admired man of letters in the Western world. A post-mortem decline in a writer's reputation is not unusual, and the question then is whether the decline is merely temporary. But in Stevenson's case what *was* unusual was the virulence of the attack on him, caused in part by the envy of less successful writers. Various aspects of Stevenson's complicated personality— the imaginative, delicate little boy of *A Child's Garden of Verses*, the gallant invalid holding the Grim Reaper at arm's length while he wrote one immortal work after another, the voyager in the South Seas—had acquired a place in the public imagination and had become so sentimentalized that they made him an easy target. Also, the profound change in manners and attitudes which took place when Victoria was no longer on the throne of England brought with it a change in literary conventions. The overpolished essays of *Virginibus Puerisque* disappeared into school textbooks; one movie version after another of *Dr. Jekyll and Mr. Hyde* turned it into a chestnut; and Stevenson has come to be thought of, by people who haven't bothered to read him, as a writer of adventure stories for boys. It seems quite possible that, given another five years—time to finish "Weir of Hermiston" and one or two other works that exist now only in brief fragments—Stevenson would have achieved the stature of, say, George Eliot (whom he in certain ways resembles), for he had come into his full powers of style and narrative vigor and his true subject matter, which lay, as it always does, close to home. A recent biographer, Ian

Bell, a Scot, has summed up the situation nicely in the introduction to his *Dreams of Exile*:

> His worship was as bizarre as the consequent neglect was unusual, and both were inspired by immense popularity. Significantly enough, the best of his peers have thought highly of Stevenson, finding qualities in the mechanisms of prose and the textures of his vision that lesser critics have missed. Others can decide if, to name three, Henry James, Jorge Luis Borges, and Graham Greene were right to put the highest value on his fiction: Stevenson's place is secure, although, as ever, there is no unanimity over what that place might be.

To my knowledge, no one has ever questioned that he belongs among the great letter writers.

The first two volumes of a new editing of Stevenson's correspondence were published this fall by Yale University Press, under the title *The Letters of Robert Louis Stevenson* ($45 each volume). There will be eight in all, and they will contain nearly twenty-eight hundred letters. Twenty-three hundred of these have been taken from the original letters, and the rest are from copies, or from a variety of printed sources, such as auction catalogues and biographies of people he wrote to. The task of collecting and photocopying the letters was begun by Bradford A. Booth, a professor of English at U.C.L.A., and after his death, in 1968, it was carried on by Ernest Mehew, a retired British civil servant, in his spare time, over twenty-five years. Mr. Mehew worked with Rupert Hart-Davis on the letters of Oscar Wilde, and should not be thought of as an amateur. His editing of the Stevenson letters is everything that could be desired. The footnotes do not overwhelm the text or, tediously, offer information that is common knowledge but, instead, provide the factual background the reader needs. And excerpts from letters written to Stevenson are given where it is important to have them. Until he reached Samoa, Stevenson rarely bothered to date his letters, but—by sifting through the newspapers of the time for events mentioned (the sailing dates of steamers and the concerts and plays Stevenson went to) and also through a great deal of other contemporary documentation, including letters to him, letters between his friends about him, his wife Fanny Stevenson's active correspondence, and his mother's pocket diaries, in which she habitually recorded his whereabouts at any given moment—Mr. Mehew has been able to date most of the letters precisely and place the rest in a reasonable context.

One would not expect the handwriting of someone whose laughter easily slid into hysteria, and who, when he was moved, threw himself onto the floor and burst into tears, to be neat and well formed. Stevenson's "u"s could not easily be distinguished from his "n"s and "v"s. Nor did he ever become a confident speller. But all these difficulties have been surmounted, and his punctuation, which he cared about, has been respected.

In these first two volumes, which cover the period from March, 1854, to July, 1879, Stevenson's main correspondents are his mother and father, his cousin Robert Alan Mowbray Stevenson, very like him in some ways, who introduced him to the primrose path, whose conversation was like a display of fireworks, and who achieved distinction as an art critic; Charles Baxter, a lawyer and a friend from university days, who acted as his business agent; Frances Sitwell, a very beautiful and intelligent Anglo-Irish woman, whom he met on a visit to England and fell in love with; Sidney Colvin, a highly respected critic of both art and literature, whom Mrs. Sitwell arranged for Stevenson to meet, and who became his mentor, and the poet and editor William Ernest Henley, whom Stevenson befriended when Henley was being treated for tuberculosis of the bone in an Edinburgh hospital, wrote plays with, and helped financially, and whose spiteful, derisive attacks both on Stevenson's writing and on his character after his death nicely illustrate the old adage "No good deed goes unpunished."

THE WHOLE WORLD knows what Stevenson looked like. The velvet coat, the long straight hair, the stringy mustache, the engaging brown eyes that were, it appears, capable of great changes of expression and color. He was five feet ten inches tall and excessively thin. This, in Edmund Gosse's words, is what it was like to make his acquaintance when he was in his mid-twenties:

> I was presented to Stevenson, at the Old Savile Club, by Mr. Sidney Colvin, who thereupon left us to our devices. We went downstairs and lunched together, and then we adjourned to the smoking-room. As twilight came on I

tore myself away, but Stevenson walked with me across Hyde Park, and nearly to my house. He had an engagement, and so had I, but I walked a mile or two back with him. The fountains of talk had been unsealed, and they drowned the conventions. I came home dazzled with my new friend.

Stevenson's earliest surviving letter was dictated to his mother when he was three years and four months old. It begins, "Dear Papa. Do come home to see me. My dear Papa will you bring a book to Mama too, I do want you to come home very soon *very*."

His parents doted on him. His father, Thomas Stevenson, was a big, solid, handsome man with a square head and broad shoulders. There was no one Stevenson loved more. When he was a child and was kept awake by night fears and fever, his father would sit at his bedside and for hours carry on a droll conversation with imaginary coachmen, innkeepers, and such, until the reassuring sound of his voice and the strangeness of what he was saying sent the little boy off to sleep.

Stevenson's mother was the daughter of a country parson and was brought up in a village four miles from Edinburgh. After Stevenson was born, she developed what was very possibly undiagnosed tuberculosis. In his early years, she rested in bed until noon, and she continued for most of her life to go to spas in England and abroad. But when she was sailing with him from island to island in the South Pacific on a ninety-five-foot schooner, she walked the deck in her starched ribbons and widow's weeds as calmly as if she were in her own parlor in Edinburgh. She outlived both her husband and her son, and when she was dying of pneumonia she thought she saw Stevenson at the foot of her bed, and exclaimed, "There is Louis! I must go."

Stevenson's health when he was a child was precarious, which meant that his schooling was often interrupted. Some winters he never went outdoors at all, and would have had a lonely childhood, except that he had fifty cousins, and those he was fondest of he met in summer at the house of his grandfather.

He didn't leave home for good until he was nearly twenty-nine, but he was always a wanderer. In his youth he explored the steep, narrow streets and dark alleys of the Old Town of Edinburgh, the harbor front, and the country roads leading away from the city until he had them by heart. When his schooling was behind him he began to go on walking trips, alone or with a friend. His cousin Bob led him to the Left Bank and to the artists' colonies in the Forest of Fontainebleau. He once amused himself by adding up the number of towns he had slept in: forty-six in England, fifty in Scotland, seventy-four in France, forty in the rest of Europe. He wrote to his mother frequently, to reassure her about his health, to keep her informed of his poste-restante address, and, if he could, to make her smile. This, from Menton:

> Do not attempt to understand the posts; it all depends on the degree of activity of the Postmaster for the moment; here, in the south, the idea of hurry about a letter is not much *répandue*. In Italy, they are still more languid.

When the Postmaster feels in the humour, he sorts a few letters and gives them to the *facteur,* and this latter delivers as many as he feels up to, very much as you might pay visits of an afternoon. It is nice to think that there are people in the world to whom life is so little serious.

In a fragment of autobiography he wrote:

I was always kept poor in my youth, to my great indignation at the time, but since then with my complete approval. Twelve pounds a year was my allowance up to twenty-three . . . and though I amplified it by a very consistent embezzlement from my mother, I never had enough to be lavish. . . . Hence my acquaintance was of what would be called a very low order; looking back upon it, I am surprised at the courage with which I first ventured alone into the societies in which I moved; I was the companion of seamen, chimney sweeps and thieves; my circle was being continually changed by the action of the police magistrate; I see now the little sanded kitchen, where . . . I . . . spent days together, generally in silence and making sonnets in a penny version book.

When he had money, he shared it with anybody who was in need of it, from close friends to street musicians and starving prostitutes. It was his habit to carry in his pockets two books, one to read and one to write in, and wherever he went he tried to find exact and appropriate words to describe what he saw. There are many passages in his early letters to his mother that look as if they had been lifted from these exercise books. In time, he learned how to capture atmosphere as well: "This morning at Swanston, the birds, poor creatures had the most troubled hour or two; evidently there was a hawk in the neighbourhood; not one sang; and the whole garden thrilled with little notes of warning and terror. I did not know before that the voice of birds could be so tragically expressive."

IN THE LATE eighteenth century, Stevenson's great-grandfather designed a system of reflector oil lamps to replace the open coal fire in the lighthouse at Kinnaird Head, on the North Sea. There were few other lights that mariners could steer by on the whole treacherous coast of Scotland. In all, he built ten new lighthouses and organized a service for manning and supplying them. Stevenson's grandfather built nearly twenty more, one of them the first ever erected far from land, on a reef that was deeply submerged at every flood tide. He invented the intermittent and flashing lights. Three of his sons, one of whom was Thomas Stevenson, continued to ring the coast with lighthouses and breakwaters.

Thomas Stevenson was the first person to use louvreboarded screens to protect meteorological instruments, and he brought the revolving holophotal light—that is to say, the arrangement of reflectors and lenses by which light is directed without perceptible loss of illumination—to something like perfection. He refused to take out patents on any of his inventions. His papers and textbooks on waves and currents and on the improvement of rivers and harbors were read all over the world, and he was often called on to testify before parliamentary committees.

It was assumed—though no one consulted his inclinations or noticed sufficiently the books he was reading—that Stevenson would follow his father into the family business. The summer before his eighteenth birthday, Stevenson was placed in harbor works on the seacoast. In a letter to his mother from Anstruther, in July, he wrote, "I am utterly sick of this grey, grim, sea-beaten hole . . . anxious to get back among trees and flowers and something less meaningless than this bleak fertility." And from Wick, in September:

> The last two days have been dreadfully hard; and I was so tired in the evenings that I could not write. . . . My hours have been 10-2 and 3-7 out in the lighter or the small boat, in a long, heavy roll from the nor'east. . . . My hands are all skinned, blistered, discoloured and engrained with tar, some of which latter has established itself under my nails in a position of such natural strength that it defies all my efforts to dislodge it. . . .
>
> The first day, I forgot to mention was like mid-winter for cold, and rained incessantly so hard that the livid white of our cold-pinched faces wore a sort of enflamed rash on the windward side.
>
> I am not a bit the worse of it, except fore-mentioned state of hands, a slight crick in my neck from the rain running down and general stiffness from pulling hauling and tugging for dear life.

There are other letters from this and the following summer, about an early form of smallpox inoculation; about a very picturesque cloud effect as the steamer was crossing the Pentland Firth; about a young man who was sentenced to forty-five days in prison for shooting ducks at Unst and hanged himself on the first day of his incarceration; about the long bleak inlet of the Fair Isle into which the flagship of the Armada was driven and how the islanders were unwilling to speak of it beyond the fact that when standing hand to hand the shipwrecked Spaniards (a great many of whom were murdered out of fear that having to feed them would result in famine) reached right across the island. They are entertaining and intelligent letters—remarkably so, considering that they were written by a boy of eighteen—but nowhere in them is there anything that would suggest an innate aptitude for engineering.

Stevenson was enrolled as an engineering student at Edinburgh University, where he made lasting friendships and practiced a kind of systematic truancy. On what he described as "a dreadful evening walk" with his father, under close questioning he broke down and confessed how little engineering he had learned and that the only thing he cared about was literature and that he wanted to be a writer. Thomas Stevenson stood up well under the blow, but to his mind writing could only be an avocation, and he proposed the study of law, for which, as it turned out, Stevenson had even less liking. This time, to satisfy his father, he stayed the course and squeaked through. He was admitted to the Scottish bar but never really practiced.

STEVENSON'S FRIENDSHIP WITH Charles Baxter was formed in tobacco shops, pubs, and low dives frequented by sailors. Baxter was stocky and outwardly phlegmatic and a master of foolery. In their letters to each other they from time to time abandoned their actual identities in favor of two imaginary, dissolute, disreputable church elders named Thompson and Johnstone, who write in broad Scots: "Dear Johnstone, I sent yon pickle siller you were speerin for yestreen. Ye're aye welcome's lang as I hae a bawbee in ma pooch. Ye ken it's no like the time we wes borrowin three penny bits o' ilk ither and no aye pying back." Underneath the nonsense, Baxter was a totally loyal, sympathetic, tactful friend—"the only person I ever knew who could *advise*," Stevenson said, "or to explain more perfectly my meaning, who could both make helpful suggestions, and at the same time hold his tongue when he had none to offer." It was to him that Stevenson turned first when he found himself in serious trouble at home:

> The thunderbolt has fallen with a vengeance now. You know the aspect of a house in which somebody is still waiting burial—the quiet step—the hushed voices and rare conversation—the religious literature that holds a temporary monopoly—the grim, wretched faces; all is here reproduced in this family circle in honour of my (what is it?) atheism or blasphemy. On Friday night after leaving you, in the course of conversation, my fa-

ther put me one or two questions as to beliefs, which I candidly answered. I really hate all lying so much now . . . but if I had foreseen the real Hell of everything since, I think I should have lied as I have done so often before. . . . I do not think I am thus justly to be called a "horrible atheist"; and I confess I cannot exactly swallow my father's purpose of praying down continuous afflictions on my head.

Thomas Stevenson was full of good sense about most things, but his Scots Presbyterian theology was fanatical, and he saw the pit opening for anyone who disagreed with him. That it should be his son made him frantic and impossible to live with. If his love for his son hadn't been so strong, he would have followed what he perceived to be the dictates of his conscience and ordered him out of the house.

To get away from remarks like "You have rendered my whole life a failure" (his father) and "This is the heaviest affliction that has ever befallen me" (his mother), Stevenson went to visit his cousin Maud Babington, who was married to a clergyman in Suffolk. Frances Sitwell was staying in the house at the time. She had recently lost her older son, and she was estranged from her husband, also a clergyman, about whose character next to nothing is known beyond the fact that he was said to be "a man of unfortunate temperament and uncongenial habits."

Cockfield Rectory was a mainly eighteenth-century house hidden from the road by elm trees and looked out on a lawn and a moat. Stevenson went there expecting croquet parties, parsons' wives, and church services, and found instead a woman whose beauty at first made him shy and then wildly talkative. He was twenty-two and she was thirty-four. In what were for him days of exquisite happiness, they took turns reading Browning aloud together, or walked in the old kitchen garden, or wandered through the meadows. She was so taken with his radiant personality and enthralling conversation that she wrote to Colvin, who was also expected at the rectory, and told him not to delay his coming. (He, too, was in love with her, and had been for some years, and eventually, after her husband died and he no longer had to support his mother, they were married.) Colvin was equally taken with Stevenson, and he later saw promise in the writing that Stevenson showed him. Between them, he and Mrs. Sitwell made Stevenson feel that his ambition to be a writer was justified. About Colvin, Stevenson would write twenty years later, "If I am what I am and where I am, if I have done anything at all or done anything well, his is the credit." Colvin wrote letters to publishers and editors, and was, as long as he lived, tireless in promoting Stevenson's interests. He read and corrected Stevenson's manuscripts—though possibly not always to their advantage, since he was something of a pedant. In any case, he stood Stevenson on his feet and got him going.

THE HUNDRED AND twenty-nine letters to Frances Sitwell are the heart of these first two volumes. They are long, long outpourings about everything but the delirium of being in love, which Stevenson was forbidden to mention, but which nevertheless he now and then does convey, indirectly:

> If I never saw you again, and lived all my days in Arabia, I should be reminded of you continually, you have gone all over the house of my mind and left everywhere sweet traces of your passage.

And:

> I have done no work today—it would not come; and I have been so sad, so sad and longed for a sight of you and the touch of your hand . . . more than I can say—more than I ever long for anything else. Did I tell you—yes I did, I remember—how I thought I saw you in the street? Do you know I wish so much to meet you by chance somewhere; I have never met you by chance; and I keep telling myself I shall see you at the next corner, and making long stories as a child does; only you never come.

In general, his letters to her are a journal of his moods, his fears, his unhappiness over the rift with his parents, and his thoughts about writing; a record of his health, his daily life, and his concern for her health and well-being; and descriptions, often brilliantly done, of the people he has met and the places he has found himself in.

Young men were always falling in love with Frances Sitwell. Her beauty and charm lasted into old age. The novelist Hugh Walpole, who was nearly fifty years younger, wrote, "There was nothing that you could not tell to her. . . . She had to the last that certain stamp of a great character, an eager acceptance of the whole of life." What she asked of Stevenson was that his feelings be those of a son rather than a lover, and you would have to be a Victorian not to find his attempts to do this cloying. At least once, the truth broke through: "I long to be with you most ardently, and I long to put my arms about your neck and kiss you, and then sit down with my head on your knees, and have a long talk, and feel you smoothing my hair: I long for all that, as one longs for—for nothing else that I can think of. And yet, that is all. It is not a bit like what I feel for my mother *here*. But I think it must be what one *ought* to feel for a mother." And then, in a postscript: "That's a lie, nobody loves a mere mother, so much as I love you, *madonna*. Before God."

Her letters to him he destroyed, as she requested, but it seems unlikely that he would have been able to write so openly to her if her letters had not conveyed a genuine fondness. Nowhere in his correspondence is there any clue to why after a couple of years the letters become less fervent and, instead, convey a lasting trust and friendship.

IN THE SUMMER of 1876, in an artists' colony at Grez, near the Forest of Fontainebleau, Stevenson met Fanny Osbourne, who was roughly the same age as Mrs. Sitwell and had come to France from California, with her children, in order to study painting. She, too, was living apart

from her husband, an amiable, handsome, incurable phi-
landerer. Though she had had a genteel upbringing in
Indianapolis, a considerable experience of the raw life in
Nevada mining camps had left its stamp on her speech
and manner. She carried her own pistol. Stevenson's description of her, written many years later in a letter to J.
M. Barrie, is "Infinitely little . . . handsome waxen face
like Napoleon's, insane black eyes, boy's hands, tiny bare
feet, a cigarette." While the painters went off to do the
medieval bridge and the poplars, she and Stevenson sat
talking hour after hour.

He went home to Edinburgh after a short while but
came to see her in Paris several times during that winter.
There are no letters to her while she remained in France
or after she returned to California in August of the following year—only discreet references to her, in letters to
one or two close friends, as "F.," or with no identification
at all. Writing to Colvin in March of 1879, Stevenson said,
"It's so long since I have written a letter that I scarce know
how. For to F. I never write letters. To begin with there's
no good. All that people want by letters has been done
between us. We are acquainted; why go on with more introductions; I cannot change so much, but she would still
have the clue and recognise every thought." The last letter in Volume II is dated (by Colvin) "28 July 1879"—just
before Stevenson set out for America to persuade her to
divorce her husband and marry him. He had published a
few stories, a number of essays, and two travel books, all
of them well received. And two-thirds of his allotted days
were spent.

STEVENSON LEFT INSTRUCTIONS that Colvin was to edit his correspondence for publication, along with a "sketch" of his life. It was not an ideal choice. Colvin was by nature somewhat dry and old-maidish. He was devoted to Stevenson's memory but had other irons in the fire. He was Keeper of Prints and Drawings at the British Museum, and there was the matter of his own literary career. Also, he was not in good health. Within the year, he published a volume of Stevenson's letters to him from Samoa, and in 1899 two more, of Stevenson's letters to his family and friends. He edited and saw through the press the twenty-eight volumes of the Edinburgh Edition. But the sketch had now become a life, and when Colvin didn't get on with it Fanny Stevenson and her son Lloyd Osbourne became so difficult to deal with that he relinquished the project to Stevenson's cousin Graham Balfour and confined his own efforts to collecting and editing the letters. By 1924, he had brought out the five volumes of correspondence that have been a part of all standard editions of Stevenson ever since.

There were, of course, many letters Colvin didn't have access to. And there was the further difficulty that most of their recipients and the persons mentioned in the letters were still living. And the question of what to do about letters containing some reference to the violent disputes over religion that had made the young Stevenson and his father and mother so unhappy. Lloyd Osbourne didn't want the events leading up to his mother's divorce to be made fully public, or the fact that she and Stevenson had been lovers before their marriage. And so on. In these matters Colvin was as courageous as circumstances permitted him to be. To Stevenson's mother he wrote,

"I would not willingly hurt you for the world . . . but if I am to handle Louis's memory at all . . . I must indicate—I hope in due proportion and with the due tenderness—the things which I know to be vitally true as to certain difficult and troubled periods of his life." Time has, as usual, disposed of all these considerations. Colvin published about eight hundred letters. To this number, two hundred and twenty letters were added in a scholarly edition of Stevenson's letters to Baxter, edited by DeLancey Ferguson and Marshall Waingrow, in 1956—the only new collection of his letters until now.

Colvin's misreadings are sometimes ludicrously wide of the mark: "box" for "fox," "cottage" for "cabbage." Sometimes part of one letter is mistakenly joined to part of another. Not all the mutilations are accidental, however. Because Colvin believed (in spite of ample evidence to the contrary) that it was what Stevenson would have wanted, he softened the profanity: "bloody" becomes "beastly," and "bugger" becomes "beggar," making no sense—but never mind. In his introduction Colvin says, "I have used the editorial privilege of omission without scruple where I thought it desirable." It is not part of the editorial privilege to omit passages without any indication that something has been left out, which Colvin did continually. Or to paste strips of paper over words the editor believes no other eyes should see. The letters to Frances Sitwell are so censored that they seem to have been written to someone who was merely a friend. When the 1899 letters appeared, Henry James, who had corresponded regularly with Stevenson over the last ten years of his life, wrote in a letter to Colvin, "One has the vague sense of omissions and truncations—one *smells* the things unprinted."

IT IS KNOWN that in 1888, as Stevenson was about to leave Saranac, he sent off in three days more than seventy letters, of which fifteen survive. When a household is being broken up, a packet of old letters is easy to toss, unexamined, on the trash fire. People who are in the habit of corresponding regularly seldom agree to save each other's letters, and if they did artificiality would very likely set in. There are over a hundred letters from the Scottish essayist, translator, and folklorist Andrew Lang to Stevenson but only half a dozen from Stevenson to Lang. And what in far too many instances the Victorians disapproved of they felt fully justified in destroying. By the middle of this century, most of Stevenson's surviving correspondence had found its way from private hands into libraries and museums, and the often idiotic censorship imposed on the published versions was at last revealed. Letters are still surfacing, but not in any quantity. More could always turn up, but the present collection is probably all there is to hope for.

In libraries the reader will find an ocean of reminiscence about Stevenson and no satisfactory biography. Third-rate writers, following the debunking fashion of the nineteen-twenties, created out of whole cloth a love affair with an Edinburgh prostitute bought off by Thomas Stevenson, or pictured Stevenson as a man so dominated by his wife that he didn't write what he longed to. All this foolishness is disposed of in J. C. Furnas's *Voyage to Windward* (1951), but the book is marred by the author's intrusive personality and condescension toward his subject. In more recent biographies one finds little that is new. The biographer's judgment tends to be unilluminating; his speculations are unconvincing or amount to psychoanalyzing of the most pedestrian kind, and are never as intelligent as Stevenson's own account of his feelings and behavior. His candor is astonishing and consistent. He did not deceive himself about his own motives or, except in moments of brief anger, those of the people around him. It could well have been Mr. Mehew's intention, through his editing of the letters and the information he has surrounded them with, to make a formal biography unnecessary.

Remembrances and reminiscences.

The photographer Consuela Kanaga, a neighbor of the Maxwells in the country. Kanaga died in 1978, and in 1992 she was given a retrospective exhibition at the Brooklyn Museum of Art.

HER VOICE WAS husky and her way of speaking unhurried. And one never knew what strange remark would come out of her mouth. "I dreamt last night that I was pursued through the treetops by a gorilla," she said sweetly, with her hand on the teapot. The tea was strong and very good, and with it there would be cookies or a loaf of Indian bread baked that afternoon. On the tea-tray was a huge jar of honey, and the mugs we drank from were iron-stone, oversize, chipped and discolored with age and use. I sat holding my mug and hoping for a story. Often they were about her growing up in San Francisco. She was her father's child. Her mother didn't understand her and continually fussed at her in an effort to make her more ladylike. This was doomed to failure. She was what she was, the ugly duckling that all artists are when young. Concession was outside her nature. Her stories about her childhood were unsentimental and haunting, and I hung on every word, feeling that this was as close to actual life as it is possible for narrative to get.

The people up and down our country road knew she was a first-rate photographer, and were fond of her personally, but rather took her for granted, and she did not go in for being Important. But once, my wife and I ran into her in a theater lobby in Greenwich Village. She was surrounded by admirers and I realized that here she was a queen.

She spoke gratefully of Edward Steichen. She loved Stieglitz and detested Georgia O'Keefe because of the way she treated him. The famous march on Selma, Ala-bama, which she took part in, recurred in her conversa-tion and was, I think, one of the high points of her life. Many years after she had focused her camera on them, she continued to love the people she had photographed: a delicate-boned little black girl holding a spray of apple blossoms to her nose. An old woman and a sickly little boy, her grandchild, in a room reeking of poverty and deprivation. And others like them.

She photographed our younger daughter when she was six days old, indoors, where the only light was what came through the windows just after the sun had gone down. The baby's face, with her eyelids covering her eyes, has the smiling inward look of a Cambodian head of Buddha. Somewhat later she photographed our older child sitting on the back steps, barelegged, in a French nursery smock, with a ragdoll in her lap and in her two-year-old face the bewilderment and grief of the dispossessed. Connie herself was dispossessed—that is to say, she was in the wrong place. The people she wanted to be photographing were in the city, in black neighborhoods, or in the deep South.

One day she brought us four lustre cups that her New England sister-in-law had given her. Family china, and very old, probably valuable, but they didn't—to use a Quaker expression—speak to her condition. And she didn't want them in her house, where there was nothing that was not of its kind rare and in some way like her or her husband, the painter Wallace Putnam. She called him Wal.

A little shining brook flows past the flagstone terrace in front of their house. It was lined on both sides with ferns, crane's bill, black-eyed Susans and wild columbine, and flowers that had gone wild, such as dark red primrose that was everywhere. She guarded the wild, natural look of the place and grieved over every weed he pulled up. She would herself have taken out only enough to bring in a little air. Flowers and weeds were not different to her.

Having in mind her photograph of a gardenia in a glass of water, I took her a white rose from our garden, in a crystal bud-vase that my wife had given me for an anniversary present. And in return got a photograph of the underside of a white seagull soaring in the upper atmosphere. Something Connie said to Wally caused him to pick up and throw at her the nearest object, which happened to be my vase with a rose in it. The seagull was by way of amends.

She had an affectionate relationship with her nephew, Marvin Brown, who lived with them for a time. Two seventeen-year-old boys of the neighborhood were attracted to her, and she taught them how to use a camera, and was worshiped by them.

At the end of her life she remarked to my wife that the cooking utensils of Eskimo women were buried with them. And added, "I know that some woman will turn up to take care of Wal, but I worry about what will happen to my pots and pans, that I have loved so."

Objects survive, and so, if proper care is taken of them, do photographs. Survive and are treasured. As I believe the work of Consuela Kanaga will be. What other photographer perceived the accumulated sorrow in the eye of a carthorse? Or that a cake of Ivory soap is of the same order of beauty as the frieze of the Parthenon?

The poet Louise Bogan, who died in February of 1970, by herself in her apartment in upper Manhattan. *The Folded Leaf* is dedicated to Bogan, because whenever Maxwell finished a chapter he sent it to her, and she encouraged him to continue. For many years the photograph of Mozart's birthplace hung in Maxwell's study in the country.

THE FIRST POETRY review that Louise Bogan did for *The New Yorker* appeared in the issue of March 21, 1931, and the last in the issue of December 28, 1968. In this magazine, between those two dates—that is to say, for thirty-eight years—poets good, bad, and indifferent came under a perceptive and just scrutiny. Out of what they did or didn't do with language she often constructed a kind of portrait of them of lasting value. Their work was also, when this was relevant, placed in a line of descent or a tradition. Aesthetic experiments were viewed with an open mind, inflation was punctured, and entrepreneurism was put in its place. At times, the exactness and lucidity of her criticism suggested that she was attempting to create a new kind of lyric poetry out of statements *about* poetry.

Louise Bogan was born in Livermore Falls, Maine. Both her parents were of Irish descent. Her father's father was a sea captain who sailed out of Portland. Though she returned to New England periodically, when she was tired and wanted to refresh her spirit, her home for most of her adult life was New York City. She lived quietly, almost anonymously, in Washington Heights, in an apartment full of books, with a photograph of Mozart's birthplace on one wall and, from a living room window, a narrow view, between apartment buildings, of the Hudson River. She published six volumes of poetry and two volumes of literary criticism. A third is now in the process of being printed. She also did a number of distinguished collaborative translations, which include Goethe's *Elective Affinities* and a selection from the *Journal* of Jules Renard.

All of the literary honors that *are* an honor to receive she received. To say that she was one of the finest lyric poets of our time is hardly to do her justice; her best poems have an emotional depth and force and a perfection of form that owes very little to the age she lived in and are not likely to go out of style, being a matter of nobody's style but her own. She was a handsome, direct, impressive, vulnerable woman. In whatever she wrote, the line of truth was exactly superimposed on the line of feeling. One look at her work—or sometimes one look at her—made any number of disheartened artists take heart and go on being the kind of dedicated creature they were intended to be. In defense of the true artist, she wrote:

> Come, drunks and drug-takers; come,
>   perverts unnerved!
> Receive the laurel, given, though late,
>   on merit; to whom
>   and wherever deserved.
>
> Parochial punks, trimmers, nice people,
>   joiners true blue,
> Get the hell out of the way of the
>   laurel. It is deathless
>   And it isn't for you.

Maeve Brennan, *The New Yorker*, 1993.

MAEVE BRENNAN DIED a few days ago, at the age of seventy-six. She was a small, charming, effortlessly witty, generous woman with green eyes, hugely oversized horn-rimmed glasses, and chestnut hair worn in a vast beehive. Her father was the Republic of Ireland's envoy to Washington, and she was brought to this country with him. She had a lovely Dublin accent. Before she came to *The New Yorker*, she was on the staff of *Harper's Bazaar*, and to be around her was to see style being invented. If you heard laughter at the water cooler, the chances were that a remark of hers had given rise to it. She began by writing about women's fashions and then moved on to doing short reviews of books. In the nineteen-fifties and sixties, those letters to the editors of Talk of the Town from the "Long Winded Lady" were all by her. They were a running diary of the city—its weather, its more fragile types, its *look*. She had a special tenderness for the seedy streets around Times Square and saw what no one else was likely to see. She published two volumes of short stories, nearly all of which appeared originally in this magazine. The best ones tend to be about a husband and wife who were not quite able to make themselves understood by each other, with the result that a kind of canopy of sadness hung over whatever happened to them. She set great store by W. B. Yeats' statement "Only that which does not teach, which does not cry out, which does not persuade, which does not condescend, which does not explain, is irresistible."

> A version of the following reminiscence of Fran-
> cis Steegmuller, delivered in April of 1995 at the
> American Academy of Arts and Letters, has been
> published and is different from this one. The public
> version is more reserved. I don't know why Maxwell
> decided to deliver the more formal version, but I
> prefer this one, which is more confiding and sounds
> more like him to me. Also, it includes material
> about Shirley Hazzard, Steegmuller's second wife,
> that isn't included in the public version.

I MET FRANCIS Steegmuller when *The New Yorker* bought
a story of his and gave it to me to edit. Since it needed
editing the way a cat needs two tails, my connection with
him remained slight. To explain what changed this I have
to go all the way around Robin Hood's barn. When Francis graduated from Columbia he went straight to Paris.
There, in the studio of the cubist painter Jaques Villon,
he met Beatrice Stein, an American girl who was Villon's
pupil. She had red hair and the warm heart that often
accompanies it. She got polio when she was an adolescent
and it left her with an atrophied leg, unable to walk without crutches. When she came of age her mother said to
her, "You can stay home and I will take care of you, or you
can go abroad on your own and have a life."

She and Francis continued to see each other when they
returned to New York and he got a job at *The New Yorker*,
writing for the Talk of the Town. But then she went off

to Vienna to study painting. Knowing that she had other suitors, Francis asked for a leave of absence but didn't explain why he wanted it. Harold Ross thought it was because he didn't care very much about the magazine and fired him. This was, of course, a stroke of good fortune, because Francis's talents lay elsewhere. He and Beatrice Stein were married in Vienna.

One evening in the mid-forties, as Francis started off to a literary cocktail party, she said to him, "I've made a beef stew. If you meet anybody there that you like talking to, bring them home to supper." Home, at that point, was a suite of small rooms in the Hotel Ansonia at Broadway and Seventy-third Street. After the introductions, Francis took my wife's coat and mine, and produced a bottle of champagne. The stew was delicious. And the four-way friendship that instantly sprang into being turned out to be lifelong.

It was impossible to know Francis and not love him. Large people tend to be good-natured and Francis was, very. I never heard him raise his voice in anger. On the other hand his disapproval was formidable, and he did not lightly put it aside. I considered him something of a dandy, for his attire on even the most ordinary occasions was spiffy. When I wrote a novel about Americans traveling in France his careful and detailed criticism was of great help to me. He was, almost from infancy, a Francophile. His mother said that before he was nine he had all but worn out the section on France in the family encyclopedia.

The French values of clarity and style and order inform everything he ever published. There was no clutter on his desk or in his study or in his mind. He typed the final manuscript of his books himself, using black typewriter ribbon for the text and red for the footnotes. Those pages I saw were elegantly typed and had no hand-written corrections.

Bea died of cancer, in 1961. Francis's grief and despair were so great that I was afraid he would never emerge from them, but after a while Fortune took pity on him. At another literary cocktail party, the Scottish novelist Muriel Spark said to him, "Francis, come with me—I want you to meet Shirley Hazzard." They were married standing in front of the fireplace of a house Francis had taken in Sharon, Connecticut, by a justice-of-the-peace, with a handful of close friends to witness the ceremony.

They were both fluent in French, and because she had a passion for Italy, he learned Italian. Their pleasure in reading, art, travel, and the company of intelligent people was heightened by being always shared. That they were very happy no one could fail to see.

In the latter part of his life they spent part of every year in Manhattan House and the rest in an 18th century villa on the outskirts of Naples, with a view across the water to Mt. Vesuvius. There was also a pied-a-terre on the nearby island of Capri. All these places had a plenitude of dictionaries of one language or another. I had an appointment with him once in the main square of the island, and to come upon him at a little table, with a cup of coffee, the *International Herald Tribune*, and a scattering of mail from America in front of him was to feel that he had arrived in Heaven slightly ahead of schedule.

The sweetness of Francis's nature is attested to by the fact that he remained on intimate terms with three highly irascible men—the novelist Graham Greene, the British art collector and critic, Douglas Cooper, and the most difficult of all, a Frenchman, the son of a provincial doctor, born in Rouen in 1821, who died in 1880, twenty-seven years before Francis was born.

Francis once remarked, "only one person stands between me and the authorship of *Madame Bovary*." I saw that he was only partly joking. That person, now residing on Mt. Parnassus, has reason to be grateful to him. What happens in Francis's translation of *Madame Bovary* is what happens when a century or more of repeated varnishings are removed from a painting and the original bright colors are once more revealed.

To appreciate the quality of his translation of Flaubert's letters, all that is necessary is to read the same letter translated by someone else. All in all, as biographer, translator, editor, annotator, and critic he served the master on eight occasions, over a period of fifty-four years. Long before this immense body of work was accomplished Francis was wearing, in the buttonhole of his lapel, the thin red ribbon of the Legion d'Honneur.

Just when one had come to think of him, because of his biographies of James Jackson Jarvis, Guy de Maupassant, and Flaubert as most at home in the 19th century, by his life of the Grand Mademoiselle he established himself with equal authority in the seventeenth; with his Mme. d'Épinay and the Abbé Galiani in the late-eighteenth century Paris and the Kingdom of Naples; with

Apollinaire and Jean Cocteau in the twentieth. Cocteau was considered to be of slight importance until Francis dealt with the quality and range of his accomplishments. The book has been mined ever since for interesting figures of the period.

The biographer deals with people frozen in time; unless he is lazy or a fool, they cannot escape him or succeed in covering their tracks. It is, needless to say, not merely a question of digging up the facts. There has to be a moral tone one can trust. In Francis's books there is no trace of the vindictive attitude toward the chosen subject that afflicts so many current biographies and that will speedily consign them to oblivion.

The Writer as Illusionist
A speech delivered at Smith College on March 4, 1955

> This speech was written during a period when Maxwell was discouraged over what he felt was a lack of public encouragement and he had thought that he might give up writing and just be an editor. In a journal he wrote,
>
> "I do not ever want to write again. I want checks to come in and requests for reprint and translation rights from every country under the sun . . .
>
> "The two subjects I have are both highly introspective and lacking in action—the man without confidence, the man who doubts his capacity to love. They are probably the same subject . . .

"Who will I take as a model, as a clue to subject matter. Not Flaubert, because I don't want it to be cold. Not Conrad, because it has to be not adventurous. The hero must be forty, and not trail along behind me. Wells, Joyce, Dostoievsky? It should have an action, and not begin with a character or a psychological difficulty . . ."

The speech consists of notes that Maxwell had been keeping for a piece of writing and a companion text that he wrote almost entirely on the train to Massachusetts. The section of instructions—"Begin with the . . ."—are the part that was written beforehand. By the time the train had arrived, he had finished the speech and decided that he liked writing too much to give up.

ONE OF THE standard themes of Chinese painting is the spring festival on the river. I'm sure many of you have seen some version of it. There is one in the Metropolitan Museum. It has three themes woven together: the river, which comes down from the upper right, and the road along the river, and the people on the riverbanks. As the scroll unwinds, there is, first, the early-morning mist on the rice fields and some boys who cannot go to the May Day festival because they have to watch their goats. Then there is a country house, and several people starting out for the city, and a farmer letting water into a field by means of a water wheel, and then more people and buildings—all kinds of people all going toward the city for the festival. And along the riverbank there are various entertainers—a magician, a female tightrope walker, several fortune-tellers, a phrenologist, a man selling spirit money, a man selling patent medicine, a storyteller. I prefer to think that it is with this group—the shoddy entertainers earning their living by the riverbank on May Day—that Mr. Bellow, Mr. Gill, Miss Chase, on the platform, Mr. Ralph Ellison and Mrs. Kazin, in the audience, and I, properly speaking, belong. Writers—narrative writers—are people who perform tricks.

Before I came up here, I took various books down from the shelf and picked out some examples of the kind of thing I mean. Here is one:

"I have just returned this morning from a visit to my landlord—the solitary neighbor that I shall be troubled with . . ."

One of two things—there will be more neighbors turning up than the narrator expects, or else he will very much wish that they had. And the reader is caught; he cannot go away until he finds out which of his two guesses is correct. This is, of course, a trick.

Here is another: *"None of them knew the color of the sky . . ."* Why not? Because they are at sea, pulling at the oars in an open boat; and so are you.

Here is another trick: *"Call me Ishmael . . ."* A pair of eyes looking into your eyes. A face. A voice. You have entered into a personal relationship with a stranger, who will perhaps make demands on you, extraordinary personal demands; who will perhaps insist that you love him; who perhaps will love you in a way that is upsetting and uncomfortable.

Here is another trick: *"Thirty or forty years ago, in one of those gray towns along the Burlington railroad, which are so much grayer today than they were then, there was a house well known from Omaha to Denver for its hospitality and for a certain charm of atmosphere."*

A door opens slowly in front of you, and you cannot see who is opening it but, like a sleepwalker, you have to go in. Another trick: *"It was said that a new person had appeared on the seafront—a lady with a dog . . .*

The narrator appears to be, in some way, underprivileged, socially. She perhaps has an invalid father that she has to take care of, and so she cannot walk along the promenade as often as she would like. Perhaps she is not asked many places. And so she has not actually set eyes on this interesting new person that everyone is talking about. She is therefore all the more interested. And meanwhile, surprisingly, the reader cannot forget the lady, or the dog, or the seafront.

Here is another trick: *"It is a truth universally acknowledged that a single man in possession of a good fortune must be in want of a wife . . ."*

An attitude of mind, this time. A way of looking at people that is ironical, shrewd, faintly derisive, and that suggests that every other kind of writing is a trick (this is a special trick, in itself) and that this book is going to be about life as it really is, not some fabrication of the author's.

So far as I can see, there is no legitimate sleight of hand involved in practicing the arts of painting, sculpture, and music. They appear to have had their origin in religion, and they are fundamentally serious. In writing—in all writing but especially in narrative writing—you are continually being taken in. The reader, skeptical, experienced, with many demands on his time and many ways of enjoying his leisure, is asked to believe in people he knows don't exist, to be present at scenes that never occurred, to be amused or moved or instructed just as he would be in real life, only the life exists in somebody else's imagination. If, as Mr. T. S. Eliot says, humankind cannot bear very much reality, then that would account for their turning to the charlatans operating along the riverbank—to the fortune-teller, the phrenologist, the man selling spirit money, the storyteller. Or there may be a different explanation; it may be that what humankind cannot bear directly it can bear indirectly, from a safe distance.

The writer has everything in common with the vaudeville magician except this: The writer must be taken in by his own tricks. Otherwise, the audience will begin to yawn and snicker. Having practiced more or less incessantly for five, ten, fifteen, or twenty years, knowing that the trunk has a false bottom and the opera hat a false top, with the white doves in a cage ready to be handed to him from the wings and his clothing full of unusual, deep pockets containing odd playing cards and colored scarves knotted together and not knotted together and the American flag, he must begin by pleasing himself. His mouth must be the first mouth that drops open in surprise, in wonder, as (presto chango!) this character's heartache is dragged squirming from his inside coat pocket, and that character's future has become his past while he was not looking.

With his cuffs turned back, to show that there is no possibility of deception being practiced on the reader, the writer invokes a time: He offers the reader a wheat field on a hot day in July, and a flying machine, and a little boy with his hand in his father's. He has been brought to the wheat field to see a flying machine go up. They stand, waiting, in a crowd of people. It is a time when you couldn't be sure, as you can now, that a flying machine would go up. Hot, tired, and uncomfortable, the little boy wishes they could go home. The wheat field is like an oven. The flying machine does not go up.

The writer will invoke a particular place: With a cardinal and a tourist home and a stretch of green grass and this and that, he will make Richmond, Virginia. He uses words to invoke his version of the Forest of Arden.

If he is a good novelist, you can lean against his trees; they will not give way. If he is a bad novelist, you probably shouldn't. Ideally, you ought to be able to shake them until an apple falls on your head. (The apple of understanding.)

The novelist has tricks of detail. For example, there is Turgenev's hunting dog, in *A Sportsman's Notebook*. The sportsman, tired after a day's shooting, has accepted a ride in a peasant's cart, and is grateful for it. His dog is not. Aware of how foolish he must look as he is being lifted into the cart, the unhappy dog smiles to cover his embarrassment. . . . There is the shop of the live fish, toward the beginning of Malraux's *Man's Fate*. A conspirator goes late at night to a street of pet shops in Shanghai and knocks on the door of a dealer in live fish. They are both involved in a plot to assassinate someone. The only

light in the shop is a candle; the fish are asleep in phos-
phorescent bowls. As the hour that the assassination will
be attempted is mentioned, the water on the surface of
the bowls begins to stir feebly. The carp, awakened by the
sound of voices, begin to swim round and round, and my
hair stands on end.

These tricks of detail are not important; they have
nothing to do with the plot or the idea of either piece of
writing. They are merely exercises in literary virtuosity, but
nevertheless in themselves so wonderful that to overlook
them is to miss half the pleasure of the performance.

There is also a more general sleight of hand—tricks
that involve the whole work, tricks of construction. Nothing that happens in Elizabeth Bowen's *The House in Paris*,
none of the characters, is, for me, as interesting as the way
in which the whole thing is put together. From that all the
best effects, the real beauty of the book, derive.

And finally there are the tricks that involve the pro-
jection of human character. In the last book that I have
read, Ann Birstein's novel, *The Troublemaker*, there is a girl
named Rhoda, who would in some places, at certain periods of the world's history, be considered beautiful, but
who is too large to be regarded as beautiful right now. It
is time for her to be courted, to be loved—high time, in
fact. And she has a suitor, a young man who stops in to
see her on his way to the movies alone. There is also a
fatality about the timing of these visits; he always comes
just when she has washed her hair. She is presented to
the reader with a bath towel around her wet head, her
hair in pins, in her kimono, sitting on the couch in the

living room, silent, while her parents make conversation with the suitor. All her hopes of appearing to advantage lie shattered on the carpet at her feet. She is inconsolable but dignified, a figure of supportable pathos. In the midst of feeling sorry for her you burst out laughing. The laughter is not unkind.

These forms of prestidigitation, these surprises, may not any of them be what makes a novel great, but unless it has some of them, I do not care whether a novel is great or not; I cannot read it.

It would help if you would give what I am now about to read to you only half your attention. It doesn't require any more than that, and if you listen only now and then, you will see better what I am driving at.

Begin with breakfast and the tipping problem.

Begin with the stealing of the marmalade dish and the breakfast tray still there.

The marmalade dish, shaped like a shell, is put on the cabin class breakfast tray by mistake, this once. It belongs in first class.

Begin with the gate between first and second class.

Begin with the obliging steward unlocking the gate for them.

The gate, and finding their friends who are traveling first class, on the glassed-in deck.

The gate leads to the stealing of the marmalade dish.

If you begin with the breakfast tray, then—no, begin with the gate and finding their friends.

And their friends' little boy, who had talked to Bernard Baruch and asked Robert Sherwood for his autograph.

The couple in cabin class have first-class accommodations for the return voyage, which the girl thinks they are going to exchange, and the man secretly hopes they will not be able to.

But they have no proper clothes. They cannot dress for dinner if they do return first class.

Their friend traveling first class on the way over has brought only one evening dress, which she has to wear night after night.

Her husband tried to get cabin-class accommodations and couldn't.

This is a lie, perhaps.

They can afford the luxury of traveling first class but disapprove of it.

They prefer to live more modestly than they need to.

They refuse to let themselves enjoy, let alone be swept off their feet by, the splendor and space.

But they are pleased that their little boy, aged nine, has struck up a friendship with Bernard Baruch and Robert Sherwood.

They were afraid he would be bored on the voyage.

Also, they themselves would never have dared approach either of these eminent figures, and are amazed that they have begotten a child with courage.

The girl is aware that her husband has a love of luxury and is enjoying the splendor and space they haven't paid for.

On their way back to the barrier, they encounter Bernard Baruch.

His smile comes to rest on them, like the beam from a lighthouse, and then after a few seconds passes on.

They discover that they are not the only ones who have been exploring.

Their table companions have all found the gate.

When the steward unlocked the gate for the man and the girl, he let loose a flood.

The entire cabin class has spread out in both directions, into tourist as well as first class.

Begin with the stealing of the marmalade dish.

The man is ashamed of his conscientiousness but worried about the stewardess.

Will she have to pay for the missing marmalade dish?

How many people? Three English, two Americans cabin class. Three Americans first class.

Then the morning on deck.

The breakfast tray still there, accusing them, before they go up to lunch.

The Orkney Islands in the afternoon.

The movie, which is shown to cabin class in the afternoon, to first class in the evening.

The breakfast tray still in the corridor outside their cabin when they go to join their friends in first class in the bar before dinner.

With her tongue loosened by liquor, the girl confesses her crime.

They go down to the cabin after dinner, and the tray is gone.

In the evening the coast of France, lights, a lighthouse.

The boat as immorality.

The three sets of people.

Begin in the late afternoon with the sighting of the English islands.

Begin with the stealing of the marmalade dish.

No, begin with the gate.

Then the stealing of the marmalade dish.

Then the luncheon table with the discovery that other passengers have been exploring and found the gate between first and second class.

Then the tray accusing them.

What do they feel about stealing?

When has the man stolen something he wanted as badly as the girl wanted that marmalade dish for an ashtray?

From his mother's purse, when he was six years old.

The stewardess looks like his mother.

Ergo, he is uneasy.

They call on their friends in first class one more time, to say goodbye, and as they go back to second class, the girl sees, as clearly as if she had been present, that some time during the day her husband has managed to slip away from her and meet the stewardess and pay for the marmalade dish she stole.

And that is why the breakfast tray disappeared.

He will not allow himself, even on shipboard, the splendor and space of an immoral act.

He had to go behind her back and do the proper thing.

A WRITER STRUGGLING—unsuccessfully, as it turned out; the story was never written—to change a pitcher of water into a pitcher of wine.

In *The Listener* for January 27th, 1955, there is a brief but wonderfully accurate description of a similar attempt carried off successfully:

"Yesterday morning I was in despair. You know that bloody book which Dadie and Leonard extort, drop by drop from my breast? Fiction, or some title to that effect. I couldn't screw a word from me; and at last dropped my head in my hands, dipped my pen in the ink, and wrote these words, as if automatically, on a clean sheet: Orlando, a Biography. No sooner had I done this than my body was flooded with rapture and my brain with ideas. I wrote rapidly till twelve . . ."

It is safe to assume on that wonderful (for us as well as her) morning, the writer took out this word and put in that and paused only long enough to admire the effect; she took on that morning or others like it—the very words out of this character's mouth in order to give them, unscrupulously, to that character; she annulled marriages and brought dead people back to life when she felt the inconvenience of having to do without them. She cut out the whole last part of the scene she had been working on so happily and feverishly for most of the morning because she saw suddenly that it went past the real effect into something that was just writing. Just writing is when the novelist's hand is not quicker than the reader's eye. She persuaded, she struggled with, she beguiled this or that character that she had made up out of whole cloth (or almost) to speak his mind, to open his heart. Day after day, she wrote till twelve, employing tricks no magician had ever achieved before, and using admirably many that they had, until, after some sixty pages, something quite serious happened. Orlando changed sex—that is, she exchanged the mind of a man for the mind of a woman; this trick was only partly successful—and what had started out as a novel became a brilliant, slaphappy essay. It would have been a great pity—it would have been a real loss if this particular book had never been written; even so, it is disappointing. I am in no position to say what happened, but it seems probable from the writer's diary—fortunately, she kept one—that there were too many interruptions; too many friends invited themselves and their husbands and dogs and children for the weekend.

Though the writer may from time to time entertain paranoiac suspicions about critics and book reviewers, about his publisher, and even about the reading public, the truth is that he has no enemy but interruption. The man from Porlock has put an end to more masterpieces than the Turks—was it the Turks?—did when they set fire to the library at Alexandria. Also, odd as it may seem, every writer has a man from Porlock inside him who gladly and gratefully connives to bring about these interruptions.

If the writer's attention wanders for a second or two, his characters stand and wait politely for it to return to them. If it doesn't return fairly soon, their feelings are hurt and they refuse to say what is on their minds or in their hearts. They may even turn and go away, without explaining or leaving a farewell note or a forwarding address where they can be reached.

But let us suppose that owing to one happy circumstance and another, including the writer's wife, he has a good morning; he has been deeply attentive to the performers and the performance. Suppose that—because this is common practice, I believe—he begins by making a few changes here and there, because what is behind him, all the scenes that come before the scene he is now working on, must be perfect, before he can tackle what lies ahead. (This is the most dangerous of all the tricks in the repertoire, and probably it would be wiser if he omitted it from his performance: it is the illusion of illusions, and all a dream. And tomorrow morning, with a clearer head, making a fresh start, he will change back the changes, with one small insert that makes all the difference.) But to continue: Since this is very close work, watch-mender's work, really, this attentiveness, requiring a magnifying glass screwed to his eye and resulting in poor posture, there will probably be, somewhere at the back of his mind, a useful corrective vision, something childlike and simple that represents the task as a whole. He will perhaps see the material of his short story as a pond, into which a stone is tossed, sending out a circular ripple; and then a second stone is tossed into the pond, sending out a second circular ripple that is inside the first and that ultimately overtakes it; and then a third stone; and a fourth; and so on. Or he will see himself crossing a long level plain, chapter after chapter, toward the mountains on the horizon. If there were no mountains, there would be no novel; but they are still a long way away—those scenes of excitement, of the utmost drama, so strange, so sad, that will write themselves; and meanwhile, all the knowledge, all the art, all the imagination at his command will be needed to cover this day's march on perfectly level ground.

As a result of too long and too intense concentration, the novelist sooner or later begins to act peculiarly.

During the genesis of his book, particularly, he talks to himself in the street; he smiles knowingly at animals and birds; he offers Adam the apple, for Eve, and with a half involuntary movement of his right arm imitates the writhing of the snake that nobody knows about yet. He spends the greater part of the days of his creation in his bathrobe and slippers, unshaven, his hair uncombed, drinking water to clear his brain, and hardly distinguishable from an inmate in an asylum. Like many such unfortunate people, he has delusions of grandeur. With the cherubim sitting row on row among the constellations, the seraphim in the more expensive seats in the *primum mobile*, waiting, ready, willing to be astonished, to be taken in, the novelist, still in his bathrobe and slippers, with his cuffs rolled back, says *Let there be* (after who knows how much practice beforehand) . . . *Let there be* (and is just as delighted as the angels and the reader and everybody else when there actually is) *Light.*

Not always, of course. Sometimes it doesn't work. But say that it does work. Then there is light, the greater light to rule the daytime of the novel, and the lesser light to rule the night scenes, breakfast and dinner, one day, and the gathering together of now this and now that group of characters to make a lively scene, grass, trees, apple trees in bloom, adequate provision for sea monsters if they turn up in a figure of speech, birds, cattle, and creeping things, and finally and especially man—male and female, Anna and Count Vronsky, Emma and Mr. Knightly.

There is not only all this, there are certain aesthetic effects that haven't been arrived at accidentally; the universe of the novel is beautiful, if it is beautiful, by virtue of the novelist's intention that it should be.

Say that the performance is successful; say that he has reached the place where an old, old woman, who was once strong and active and handsome, grows frail and weak, grows smaller and smaller, grows partly senile, and toward the end cannot get up out of bed and even refuses to go on feeding herself, and finally, well cared for, still in her own house with her own things around her, dies, and on a cold day in January the funeral service is read over her casket, and she is buried. . . . Then what? Well, perhaps the relatives, returning to the old home after the funeral, or going to the lawyer's office, for the reading of the will.

In dying, the old woman took something with her, and therefore the performance has, temporarily at least, come to a standstill. Partly out of fatigue, perhaps, partly out of uncertainty about what happens next, the novelist suddenly finds it impossible to believe in the illusions that have so completely held his attention up till now. Suddenly it won't do. It might work out for some other novel but not this one.

Defeated for the moment, unarmed, restless, he goes outdoors in his bathrobe, discovers that the morning is more beautiful than he had any idea—full spring, with the real apple trees just coming into bloom, and the sky the color of the blue that you find in the sky of the West Indies, and the neighbors' dogs enjoying themselves, and the neighbor's little boy having to be fished out of the brook, and the grass needing cutting—he goes outside thinking that a brief turn in the shrubbery will clear his mind and set him off on a new track. But it doesn't. He comes in poorer than before, and ready to give not only this morning's work but the whole thing up as a bad job, ill advised, too slight. The book that was going to live, to be read after he is dead and gone, will not even be written, let alone published. It was an illusion.

So it was. So it is. But fortunately we don't need to go into all that because, just as he was about to give up and go put his trousers on, he has thought of something. He has had another idea. It might even be more accurate to say another idea has him. Something so simple and brief that you might hear it from the person sitting next to you on a train; something that would take a paragraph to tell in a letter . . . Where is her diamond ring? What has happened to her furs? Mistrust and suspicion are followed by brutal disclosures. The disclosure of who kept after her until she changed her will and then who, finding out about this, got her to make a new will, eight months before she died.

The letters back and forth between the relatives hint at undisclosed revelations, at things that cannot be put in a letter. But if they cannot be put in a letter, how else can they be disclosed safely? Not at all, perhaps. Perhaps they can never be disclosed. There is no reason to suspect the old woman's housekeeper. On the other hand, if it was not a member of the family who walked off with certain unspecified things without waiting to find out which of the rightful heirs wanted what, surely it could have been put in a letter. Unless, of course, the novelist does not yet know the answer himself. Eventually, of

course, he is going to have to let the cat—this cat and all
sorts of other cats—out of the bag. If he does not know,
at this point, it means that a blessing has descended on
him, and the characters have taken things in their own
hands. From now on, he is out of it, a recorder simply
of what happens, whose business is with the innocent
as well as with the guilty. There are other pressures than
greed. Jealousy alone can turn one sister against the other,
and both against the man who is universally loved and
admired, and who used, when they were little girls, to
walk up and down with one of them on each of his size-
12 shoes. Things that everybody knows but nobody has
ever come right out and said will be said now. Ancient
grievances will be aired. Everybody's character, including
that of the dead woman, is going to suffer damage from
too much handling. The terrible damaging facts of that
earlier will must all come out. The family, as a family, is
done for, done to death by what turns out in the end
to be a surprisingly little amount of money, considering
how much love was sacrificed to it. And their loss, if the
novelist really is a novelist, will be our gain. For it turns
out that this old woman—eighty-three she was, with a
bad heart, dreadful blood pressure, a caricature of herself,
alone and lonely—knew what would happen and didn't
care; didn't try to stop it; saw that it had begun under her
nose while she was still conscious; saw that she was the
victim of the doctor who kept her alive long after her will
to live had gone; saw the threads of will, of consciousness,
slip through her fingers; let them go; gathered them in
again; left instructions that she knew would not be fol-

lowed; tried to make provisions when it was all but too late; and then delayed some more, while she remembered, in snatches, old deprivations, an unwise early marriage, the absence of children; and slept; and woke to remember more—this old woman, who woke on her last day cheerful, fully conscious, ready for whatever came (it turned out to be her sponge bath)—who was somehow a symbol (though this is better left unsaid), an example, an instance, a proof of something, and whose last words were—But I mustn't spoil the story for you.

At twelve o'clock, the novelist, looking green from fatigue (also from not having shaved), emerges from his narrative dream at last with something in his hand he wants somebody to listen to. His wife will have to stop what she is doing and think of a card, any card; or be sawed in half again and again until the act is letter-perfect. She alone knows when he is, and when he is not, writing like himself. This is an illusion, sustained by love, and this she also knows but keeps to herself. It would only upset him if he were told. If he has no wife, he may even go to bed that night without ever having shaved, brushed his teeth, or put his trousers on. And if he is invited out, he will destroy the dinner party by getting up and putting on his hat and coat at quarter of ten, causing the other guests to signal to one another, and the hostess to make a mental note never to ask him again. In any case, literary prestidigitation is tiring and requires lots of sleep.

And when the writer is in bed with the light out, he tosses. Far from dropping off to sleep and trusting to the fact that he did get home and into bed by ten o'clock after all, he thinks of something, and the light beside his bed goes on long enough for him to write down five words that may or may not mean a great deal to him in the morning. The light may go on and off several times before his steady breathing indicates that he is asleep. And while he is asleep he may dream—he may dream that he had a dream in which the whole meaning of what he is trying to do in the novel is brilliantly revealed to him. Just so the dog asleep on the hearthrug dreams; you can see, by the faint jerking movement of his four legs, that he is after a rabbit. The novelist's rabbit is the truth—about life, about human character, about himself and therefore by extension, it is to be hoped, about other people. He is convinced that this is all knowable, can be described, can be recorded, by a person sufficiently dedicated to describing and recording, can be caught in a net of narration. He is encouraged by the example of other writers—Turgenev, say, with his particular trick of spreading out his arms like a great bird and taking off, leaving the earth and soaring high above the final scenes; or D. H. Lawrence, with his marvelous ability to make people who are only words on a page actually reach out with their hands and love one another; or Virginia Woolf, with her delight in fireworks, in a pig's skull with a scarf wrapped around it; or E. M. Forster, with his fastidious preference for what a good many very nice people wish were not so.

But what, seriously, was accomplished by these writers or can the abstract dummy novelist I have been describing hope to accomplish? Not life, of course; not the real thing;

not children and roses; but only a facsimile that is called literature. To achieve this facsimile the writer has, more or less, to renounce his birthright to reality, and few people have a better idea of what it is—of its rewards and satisfactions, or of what to do with a whole long day. What's in it for him? The hope of immortality? The chances are not good enough to interest a sensible person. Money? Well, money is not money any more. Fame? For the young, who are in danger always of being ignored, of being overlooked at the party, perhaps, but no one over the age of forty who is in his right mind would want to be famous. It would interfere with his work, with his family life. Why then should the successful manipulation of illusions be everything to a writer? Why does he bother to make up stories and novels? If you ask him, you will probably get any number of answers, none of them straightforward. You might as well ask a sailor why it is that he has chosen to spend his life at sea.

A preface.

> Preface to the Quality Paperback Book Club edition of three novels—*Time Will Darken It*, *The Chateau*, and *So Long, See You Tomorrow*. The story Maxwell describes as the original version of *So Long, See You Tomorrow*, can be found in *Maxwell: Later Novels and Stories*, edited by Christopher Carduff and published by the Library of America.

TIME WILL DARKEN IT was begun in the summer of 1945, shortly after I was married, and I had had the feeling that, for someone as happy as I was, writing was not possible, but one day, habit reasserting itself, I sat down at the typewriter and began describing an evening party in the year 1912. It took place in the house I lived in as a child. I seemed to have no more choice about this than one has about the background of a dream. I also hadn't any idea about what was going to happen to the characters. The evening simply unfolded moment by moment until it was time for the guests to rise and say *Good-night* . . . *Good night* . . .

The next day, when I returned to my typewriter, there they all were waiting for me. In a way that had never happened before and has never happened again, the story advanced by set conversations. A, who was late to work, had to stop and deal with the large wet tears of B, C tried unsuccessfully to reach out to D at the breakfast table, but E, who is older and wiser about people, managed to . . . as if I were writing a play. When I started a new chapter it was a matter of figuring out which of them hadn't talked to each other lately. When my judgment faltered—usually around lunchtime—I would take what I had written and read it to my wife, sitting outside on the grass.

Why the Mississippi relatives? They were simply *there*. I knew that the party was given for them when I sat down to write about it. When I was a little boy my mother and father had a visit of some duration from my Grandmother Maxwell's sister and her family, who came north from Greenville, Mississippi, to escape the heat. Their syntax, their soft Southern way of speaking, the intensely personal interest they brought to any social encounter made them seem very different from the Middle Westerners I was used to. They charmed everyone they came in contact with, but the resemblance of the Mississippi characters in the novel to my flesh-and-blood relatives went no farther than that. As a rule, unless real people have suffered a sea change and become creatures of the novelist's imagination, the breath of life is not in them.

Some novels don't require much in the way of a setting, if the interior or exterior dialogue is sufficiently compelling. This story, I felt, needed things for the eye to rest on. Houses all up and down a quiet street. Hitching posts. Elm trees arching over the brick pavement. Sounds, too: the ice cream wagon, the locust and the katydid. And smells from the kitchen or the pigpen. So I surrounded the characters with the summer and winter of a small town set in farmland so flat that, once you have left the outskirts behind you, you can see in every direction all the way to the horizon. Or, to put it differently, the book needed as much poetry as prose fiction can accommodate without becoming too fancy.

Though the characters were so talkative, there was one subject they were reticent about, and I had to decide for myself whether or not Austin King was unfaithful to his marriage vows. I tried it both ways, with the result that the novel went off simultaneously in two directions, and I followed each one for a considerable distance before I finally decided that he probably would not have allowed himself to sleep with his young cousin, much though he may have wanted to. He kept himself always on a very short rein.

Some readers have understood the last chapter to mean that the Kings' marriage was finished. This was not my intention. In the year 1912, in a town like Draperville, women did not leave their husbands except in fear for their life. Lying awake in the dark Martha King threw the book at Austin in order to prepare herself to forgive him.

Before the First World War, when it was the best time to go to France, I went to islands, instead—Bermuda, Trinidad, Barbados, Martinique. When I finally did go to Europe, in the summer of 1948, it was to please my wife, who had been taken to France and England by her parents when she was twelve years old and wanted to see again places and things she remembered. To me, France was the tragedies of Racine, Proust's madeleine, *Le Grand Meaulnes*, *The Counterfeiters*, and Cyrano de Bergerac's white plume. I did not expect to feel any different toward the country of France than I would feel toward, say, the state of Texas, but at first sight of the coastline, before I ever set foot on French soil, I lost my heart. It didn't occur to me to hope that this attachment would be returned. Nevertheless we fairly often met with an affectionate response—from the cook and the concierge of the Hotel Montgomery in Pontorson, from a waiter in a small restaurant in the St. Sulpice quarter of Paris, from an old woman in the Touraine, and so on.

We wandered from place to place, drunk on the beauty of a country so much older than the U.S.A., and looked at every public building, every faded tricolour, every village street, every ticket-taker, every flame-eater, every boulangerie, every patisserie, every cremerie, as if our lives depended on seeing all that there was to see. It's a wonder we didn't go blind. Because of all they had lived through during the German occupation and because we were among the first post-war American tourists, the French were open and accessible in a way that was not, I think, usual with them.

After four months our money ran out. I walked into our house on a country road forty miles north of New York City, put the suitcases down, and with my hat still on my head sat down to my typewriter and wrote a page of notes for a novel. I thumbtacked it to the bookcase behind me and didn't look at it again. For the next ten years I lived in my own private France, which I tried painstakingly to make real to the reader. It was my way of not coming home.

The Javanese stone-carvers who somewhere around the year A.D. 800 covered the Borobudur with scenes in high relief and statues of the Buddha, enshrined in openwork bells, intended to delineate symbolically the material world and all human life, sometimes called The Thousand and One Things. I thought this was a worthy goal to aim at, though in a novel whose action contained nothing more dramatic than hurt feelings caused by misapprehension and a failure to understand the language, it would probably not be noticed. After the book was done I looked for the first time at the sheet of paper I had tacked to the bookcase and saw to my surprise that everything on it was disposed of in the book.

When I turned the manuscript over to the publisher, one of the readers felt strongly that Part II was unnecessary and should be cut. From the point of view of classical form he was, I suppose, right, but it would have left a number of questions unanswered. Also there is, there has to be, a form inherent in the material, and it doesn't always follow the ideas of Aristotle or even Henry James. Losing my confidence I turned to Alfred Knopf, who was sitting on the sidelines during the discussion, and he said, "Have it whatever way you want."

So I let it stand. I would not now be able to forgive myself if I hadn't.

WHEN I WAS in the seventh or eighth grade the father of a boy in my class at school committed a murder. It was not a thing you could easily forget. The details floated around in my mind and were considerably altered, as is likely to happen with a memory carried over a period of many years. The first time I tried to deal with the situation in writing, it was in the form of a short story in which a boy was wakened out of a deep sleep by the sound of a gun going off inside the house. It was still dark outside. He heard his mother's voice saying "Don't!" and a second shot and then silence. He thought his father was away and that he was the nearest thing to a man in the house and must protect his mother. When he opened the door of his room the hall light was on and his father was standing there as if lost in thought. Indicating the room where he and the boy's mother slept he said, "Don't go in there." After which he went from room to room turning on lights and opening and shutting drawers, and when finally he left, the boy summoned the strength to telephone his grandmother and say, "You have to come." "Can't it wait until morning?" she asked and he said, "No." He was waiting on the front steps when she got there, and told her about the shots and that his father had said he was not to go in the bedroom. "Somebody's got to do it," she said. The milkman making his rounds in his wagon in the first morning light saw them, the old woman and the boy, standing on the sidewalk, and heard the old woman's story and took him in his wagon to the police station. It was all very real to me, but when *The New Yorker* didn't cotton to it I concluded that I didn't have the kind of literary talent that can deal at close hand with raw violence, and put the manuscript in a drawer. One day, sitting at my desk, I found myself thinking of the boy in my class, the murderer's son, and how we met in the corridor of a high school in Chicago, and I saw there was the possibility of a novel. I remembered reading about the murder in the *Lincoln Evening Courier* but it turned out that their files did not go back that far. My cousin Tom Perry, who lives in Lincoln, got photocopies for me from the state historical society, and I was astonished to discover how far, in that short story, I had strayed from the facts. I have not departed from them in any way in *So Long, See You Tomorrow*. What I couldn't find in the newspaper account or what nobody could tell me, I have permitted myself to imagine, but the reader is given fair notice that I am doing this.

Christopher Isherwood once observed that in a novel the first person narrator must be as solidly done as the other characters or there will be an area of unreality. One can think of exceptions—*The Brothers Karamazov*, for example—but anyway I thought he had something. If I followed his precept it meant that I had two stories on my hands, which must somehow be made into one. Since any prose narrative is open, during the writing of it, to all the winds that blow—to anything that happens to the novelist, to what he happens to read, to any new idea that comes into his head—it is likely to be affected in some degree by accident. One day, waking from a nap, I sat on the edge of the bed in a mild daze, staring at a row of books. Among them was a book about Alberto Giacometti. I opened it at random and found myself reading a letter from Giacometti to Matisse in which he described a love affair that took place while he was working on a piece of sculpture now known as "Palace at 4 A.M." As literal autobiography I doubt if it is worth much, but it contains a perfect metaphor for what I wanted to say and a bridge between the two stories that made them hold together.

I came to have a considerable feeling for the farm boy whose character and daily life I invented. The actual boy who served as a model for him I knew only very slightly. After the novel was published I wondered if he (now, of course, an elderly man) would read it. Or if I would hear from him. I never did.

PART IV

PRIVATE LIFE

A note on the Maxwells.

Emmy is Emily Maxwell, Maxwell's wife. They were married in 1945 and died within days of each other, in 2000. Kate and Brookie are their daughters. The Maxwells' first apartment with their children was at 1 Gracie Square, and their second was a few blocks away, at 544 East 86th Street. Both buildings were beside the East River. Maxwell loved the Gracie Square apartment, and never wanted to leave it, but the building went co-op, one of the earlier buildings in the city to do so. The lawyer for *The New Yorker*, whose judgment Maxwell trusted, told him that co-op buildings were a fad and that he would regret investing in one. For the rest of his life Maxwell regretted not buying the apartment. The Maxwells died, Emily on July 23, 2000, and Maxwell on July 31, at the East 86th Street apartment.

1966

IT IS STILL warm, still summer in New York, with the windows still open and the night sometimes breathless, and occasionally wind comes up, forcing us to close the windows and warning us of storms that are coming down the East River this winter. Emmy has discovered that from eight stories up you can tell exactly how much money people have, the people who walk down East End Avenue. It's quite true. You can't see whether they are happy or unhappy, kind or selfish, stupid or clever, but you can see their financial status. In a dozen different ways it shines out. On the other hand you can tell if the dogs are happy or unhappy, kind or selfish, stupid or clever. The poodles are way ahead, on all counts.

1959

WE ARE NOW under a blanket of snow. Kate said yesterday morning as I was dressing her—apropos Brookie's being my delight (Kate is officially her mother's delight) and she, Kate, my treasure—"Will I be your treasure when I am old and tired and dead and gone?" And I said, after a moment's reflection devoted mostly to who was going to be old and tired and dead and gone before whom, "Yes, I think you will be," and it seemed to me, by the way her face cleared, after a moment's reflection devoted to she didn't say what, that she was reassured by this statement. Probably she knows better, but had heard what she wanted to hear. And of course it is true, or would be, if it were possible.

1976

KATE IS HOME all week. On the strength of her saying that she might be here tomorrow I got tickets to Leontyne Price and the Berlin Philharmonic, and what they are doing is the Brahms German Requiem. It is the first time that we have gone to a concert together in years. She and Shahabuddin[2] and his family are going to Turkey at the beginning of December, for a religious festival built around whirling dervishes. Sometimes she says things that are her deepest convictions, newly arrived at, and that are also mine, but that I know I have never expressed to her. I listen with my mouth open, in amazement . . .

1973

A WEEK AGO today, Wednesday, Kate dreamt that a child was killed and there were people standing around grieving over it. Friday night when we went to the country we learned that, the day before, Linda Sternau's child fell off a slide and landed on her head and died. The repairman came on Saturday to fix the ailing refrigerator just as Emmy and I were walking out of the house to go to the funeral, but Larry[3] took over and we went on. The service was in the Baptist Church, which is circa 1840, and plain and small, with a small country graveyard dating back to before the Revolution. All my handkerchiefs were in town, but I had taken a square of white percale from the rag bag and some kleenex. The minister was not as offensive as some, but I could barely contain my impatience with him. The very small coffin at the foot of the pulpit was covered

---

2 A Sufi teacher with whom Kate was studying.
3 Brookie's boyfriend.

with a patchwork quilt of about the same age as the church. I gave the percale to Emmy and did with the kleenex. When the minister had finished preaching he announced that the child's mother was going to say something. She's perhaps twenty-two, and blonde. Both grandparents are handsome and so is she: German refugees from the Thirties. She had hardly opened her mouth when I forgot how to breathe, and raised the kind of commotion people do who are trying not to choke to death while simultaneously not raising a commotion. She stood there talking about the baby, with her father and mother and brother standing beside her, the only people in the church who were not weeping. Her courage was unbearable. It was not a day for being spared. The snow is coming down exactly the way it did on the day of my mother's funeral, and as we stood uphill from the open grave I hid behind the backs of taller people so the family wouldn't see me shedding tears. The child's father had gone off somewhere about a year after she was born and never come back, and the grandfather had moved in and taken his place. All last summer we saw them together at the Sternau's swimming pool: the passion of a man of forty-five for a child of three. And there he was standing by the grave while the child's mother stepped forward and dropped a rose into the hole, and the snow turned his hair gray in front of my eyes. A year from now, six months from now, we will go swimming in their pool, and he will smile and be polite as only a German refugee from the Thirties can be, and it will be as if the child had never existed. But he will never be young again. I saw it happen, in the falling snow.

Undated

WHEN EMMY AND I were married we went immediately
to my house in the country (where, though it is altered
beyond recognition we still live much of the time) and it
was raining. We sat on either side of the fire, reading. For
the last six months we had been struggling constantly to
get to one another, or perhaps it would be more accurate
to say that for six months *I* had been struggling to get to
where she was and to persuade her that she was happy
where I was, but at all events she was persuaded. We
had stood up in church and announced our intentions,
and here we were and it was cold and raining and somehow not what it had been before or what we expected.
That is to say, it had an aspect of all eternity. We were
polite. But both secretly alarmed. And on the third day
the sun came out and we both closed our books at the
same moment and got up and went about doing things,
in the kitchen, in the garden, and that was the end of all
eternity, thank God.

The first week we were married, Emmy filled a bushel
basket with my prescriptions and emptied them into the
garbage can. I was too horrified to protest. And to myself
said, Well, in time, I will get them all refilled and replaced.
But never had occasion to, or even to try to, since it turned
out that they were one and all specifics against the lonely
celibate life.

1965

> On November 9, a Tuesday, there was a blackout in
> New York City and much of the East Coast.

IF I HAD left the office when I intended to, I should have
spent five hours standing up in a crowded subway train
somewhere between Grand Central and 86th Street,
and been rescued by firemen with flashlights. As it was,
Milton Greenstein came by with a question concerning
something I should have done that had been left undone,
and it took me a time to remember the details and offer
the proper apologies and excuses, and so it was about five-
twenty when I descended the stairs to the level of the
subway platforms. I saw at a glance that something was
wrong; there were too many people on the platform, and
this always means a delay in the trains. But my feet carried
me on down the stairs and I joined the other people there,
and then heard a voice speaking over the public-address
system (so low that it was like a thought in my head) this
beautiful sentence: "There is no power in all the subway."
We looked at one another, and then my native selfishness
asserted itself, and I thought if all these people start to
get on the Third Avenue bus there will be a lot of crowd-
ing and pushing, so I hop-footed it right up the stairs. (I
was at the head of the platform, where it is less crowded
as a rule. If I have been in the center, I could not possibly have left because of people pouring down the stairs.
And when, five minutes later, the lights went out, people

began to scream and push, and there was all the makings of panic. But, I read in the paper the next day, some man flicked his cigarette lighter and held it up, and this one small gleam reminded others that they had matches and lighters in their pockets, and so, instead of trampling one another to death they lighted themselves out into the open air.) On the stairs, with other people in close pursuit, I met streams of people coming down, and the ones coming up shouted "No power!" cheerfully to the newcomers, who continued right on down while they thought about this information. Along the street everything was normal and I dogtrotted the one long block to Third Avenue, decided which was the bus corner, and went and stood there, in a group of perhaps a dozen people. And suddenly it happened. It was rapid but not instantaneous. It was exactly like the closing of an eyelid. The darkness didn't nearly come, it came down. From above. Perhaps the power failed first on the upper floors of the skyscrapers, but I can only guess, because as it happened I had such a massive surge of adrenaline in my knees. (Emmy and the children uptown, and I in this canyon, unable to reach them or take care of them, and *How could it be happening?*) At that point a lighted box came along—the Third Avenue bus, totally empty, and we began to crowd and push to get on. When I had got my change and picked up my briefcase from the floor I looked around and saw that one of my colleagues was already sitting in the middle of the bus and was motioning for me to come and join him. It was a youngish reporter named Jeremy Bernstein, the brother of the conductor, and we had left *The New Yorker* office at the same time. Riding down in the elevator, after a nod at each other, I had racked my brain for a conversational remark and decided I would probably never have anything to say to him. Well, I sat down and we didn't stop talking for the next forty minutes. I now consider him among my dear friends, though I haven't seen him since. He kept looking to see, as we passed an intersection, if the lights were on in Brooklyn and Queens and Jersey (they were on in Jersey but we couldn't see that far) and I kept seeing lights high up in apartment houses and being sure they were too bright for a candle. They were candles. I was and I'm still astonished at how exactly like a good deed in a naughty world the light of one candle shines. Meanwhile, at the street level, visions. The vision of a Horn and Hardart automat lighted only by candles. The vision of a movie theater marquee, wholly dark, but with human faces in the darkness. As the bus moved uptown slowly we were aware that there were no stoplights at the intersections. It was like drifting down stream in a canoe. And lighted cars (many of them had their interior lights on) kept sweeping past us. And where were we? 49th? 53rd? From time to time a voice would call out the street, learned from a quick glance, by the light of some car. The bus filled and emptied and filled again, over and over. There were policeman at intersections (but not at every intersection) with flashlights, guiding traffic. The visions continued. And so did the speculations, which got easier and less fearful with every moment that we were still unannihilated . . . an English girl said No, it wasn't at all like the Blitz: Then you knew what to expect, but this was eerie and she was frightened . . . Less and less frightened I arrived at 85th Street, parted company with my companion, and stepped down into an atmosphere that was enchanted. Everywhere people were going quietly about their business in the dark. It was like another planet, where the sky, instead of being blue in the daytime, is black. I went into a corner bar to get a pack of matches to light my way up sixteen flights of stairs and found myself in a de la Tour. The bar was C-shaped, with the bartender inside the C, and in front of every man standing around it was a glass of beer and a lighted candle, throwing light up into his face from below. I have seldom seen anything more beautiful. In daylight, the following day, I saw the same place and was unable to determine the elements out of which the beauty had been arrived at. It was a plain uninteresting German bar, on a corner of Yorkville. After the first block, going East from Lexington, people began to thin out. Walking along beside a Puerto Rican messenger boy I asked if he minded if I listen to his transistor radio. I was cordially invited to, and so learned that it wasn't just New York City but the whole Eastern seaboard. (Learned erroneously: it was only the northeastern part of the United States and a little of Canada.) In the next block the tall young woman walking ahead of me suddenly began to run—having decided that she was afraid of dark doorways? Or of me? In the block after that, I realized that there was somebody walking behind me, and atavistic impulses of self-protection made me keep turning my head, and politeness kept me from turning it far enough to see how close the person was, or what he might be intending. In the final block I saw the moon rising over the river, bringing an end to the darkness. The super and the elevator man were in the lobby, and offered a flashlight but I declined, having my matches, and started up the stairs by the back elevator. To save my life I could not keep straight where I was, but when I reached the fourth the kitchen door opened and a Negro cook with a lovely big plain face held a lighted candle out for me to see my way by, and told me what floor it was. On the floor above, the door opened again, and it was a little boy with a flashlight. And so on, until I reached the eighth and there was Lillie Mae and the children. Ours and the two from next-door, whom they knew only slightly until this evening, and now has become friends with. (Six nights later I went to a meeting at Brearley to hear a talk by Brookie's teacher, and saw her school notebook, the last page of which described my homecoming. The title of the essay was,

My Current Event
The First Power Failure

It seems I walked in and shouted "There are no lights all over the whole Eastern Seaboard from Canada to Miami, Florida!" And that they then rushed into the next apartment and shouted "THERE ARE NO LIGHTS ALL OVER!" etc. Emmy was in the living room, and terribly happy to see me, and I made us a drink, and we had dinner, and then stood at the living room window. The radio had asked people to stay off the streets, and it seemed a good idea, in a city famous for its muggings, but actually the crime rate went down that night. The only explanation I have heard that makes any sense is Mary Cheever's. She said that possibly criminals are afraid of the dark. The East River shown bright silver, like a poem by de la Mare, and the whole of Eighty-sixth Street was white with moonlight. The moon was huge, and lasted all evening. And looking down at the house across the street where, twenty years ago, Emmy and I were eating wedding cake and drinking champagne, I saw a man and then another man pass along the sidewalk, under the trees, and thought, Is it a man or a werewolf? And all evening a police car with a revolving red and white roof light went back and forth across the Hell's Gate Bridge. Then suddenly it wasn't there anymore. I put down papers for Daisy in the study, the way I used to do when she was a puppy and not allowed in the street because she hadn't had her final shots, and the fastidious creature wouldn't use them. We went to bed, the children having done their homework with the children from next-door, around our dining room table, by candlelight and in costume. The little boy had on a green velour hat with a white plume that I had mistakenly urged Emmy to buy in Paris in 1948 (it rose on her forehead, being too small for her) and a wine-colored and silk cape that belonged to E's Aunt Betty, and looked like one of the heroes of *The Children of the New Forest*. Kate was Elizabeth I, the other neighbor's child was, I think, Mary Queen of Scots, and Brookie must have been, though I don't remember, Helen Keller. Who else would she be? The next door report was that the lights would come on at ten, and they didn't. When I woke at three and saw that there were no festoons of lights on Hell's Gate Bridge, only the two red, oil-fed, I suppose, beacons at the top of the pylons, I began to worry—about food, water, everything. At six-twenty I opened my eyes and saw the festoons of lights were lighted. And closed my eyes again, and through closed eyelids, five minutes later, saw the lights in our bedroom come on. The children were heartbroken.

1964

A summer vacation.

A NICE BIG—almost huge—house right on the ocean, in a place that has slyly kept itself unchanged (except that eleven houses were swept into the sea by a big storm and the ocean is steadily eating away at the beach) since 1922. The cretonnes were pleasantly faded, the white wicker chairs and sofas all had a list to port or starboard, and the walls were painted white or Wedgewood blue or moss green, instead of that depressing brown varnish. Upstairs, rooms opening out of rooms opening out of rooms, and the waves breaking such a small distance away that at night I felt myself raised, softly, mattress and all, and then deposited again, just as softly. But the seashore is so full of tricks. We all dreamt wildly, night after night.

One very curious thing happened. We had company for Sunday lunch and were standing on the upstairs porch when to my astonishment I saw a scene out of the Old Testament: the Crossing of the Red Sea. Only they weren't crossing it but walking on the shore. A mile long string of people, walking closely together in twos and threes, as if the town of Cherry Grove had decided to move to Ocean Beach. I cannot tell you how strange it was, until Emmy perceived the explanation. Beyond the Israelites, in the water, an arm raised and disappeared, and another and another. It was a long distance swimming match, and the spectators were keeping abreast of it on foot.

We went to church, by way of protective coloration, "for the children," and I discovered that when my mind decided once and for all that there wasn't a word of truth in it, my heart wasn't consulted. That is to say, I love singing hymns, I am elevated by the language of the ritual, I was even interested in the sensation of being preached to.

1971

ANOTHER CAT MIGHT be the better for a good home and we would be better for having another cat but Daisy* wouldn't. Tupelo always adored her and used to sleep curled up inside Daisy's legs. While Tupelo was a kitten Daisy accepted him, but when he became half grown and endlessly diverting, when he was allowed to sleep on the bed while I was taking a nap and other favors without number that were denied to The Dog, a deterioration of personality set in that was appalling. The Persian princess turned into a lunk, without life, without enthusiasm, without anything on her mind but getting to the cat's dish to steal food out of it when nobody was looking. She conveyed her despair in other ways, such as puddles on the living room rug. She has only two or three more years to live, and it seems better, since she has already reverted to her old charming self, not to make her suffer the pangs of jealousy again. The real trouble was that the jealousy was well-founded . . .

*A yellow Labrador.

1969

A demonstration against the Vietnam War, attended by Maxwell, Emily, Kate, and Brookie.

WE ENDED UP on W. 49th St., inside of the cathedral steps, holding our lighted candles. All of Fifth Avenue was *paved* with people, sitting peacefully on the pavement holding candles and singing. Sometimes we sat and sometimes, when the view was obstructed, stood. I made the girls put their long hair inside their coats, because of the candles at their backs. My raincoat still has wax tears on it, which I can't bear to have removed. At one point silence began to emanate from somewhere, on whose instructions I don't know, and it grew and grew and spread all through the crowd. I can't tell you how marvelous it was to hear thousands of people being silent with their arms aloft in the V symbol, and their faces lighted by candles. And such beautiful faces. Mostly young, but not all. Some rough boys said sweetly to Kate, "Where can we buy candles?" and *snap* went three candles. It was like Woodstock without the drugs. Or the mud. But at one point some people in front of us started to leave and some people behind us were trying to get closer, and I saw why Emmy doesn't like crowds. She and Edith were swept away, and I just managed barely to keep the children together and get them into a less crowded spot.

Later that night there were candlelight processions here, there, and everywhere. At ten minutes after one, Emmy and I were wakened out of a sound sleep and went to the window and saw a parade coming down 86th street, which is very wide, and coming fast. By the time I had got the children out of their beds it was under our windows. Students, mostly men, but girls too, carrying candles and torches and singing and in such a good humor, but also coming so fast, and with such purpose and *force*. I never saw anybody march that way before. It was revolutionary, though it ended up peacefully in front of the Mayor's house, two blocks north of us. I cannot tell you how moving it was. It made me feel that that's what the streets are for.

1971

JUST WHEN I was running back and forth on the highwire with little cat steps, balancing the card table, the umbrella, the dinner plate, the pitcher of wine, and the red rubber ball, and thinking this is something to be doing all at once, I got a summons for jury duty. I have served briefly on a case involving a heroin pusher, which stopped abruptly when the pusher in question settled for a lesser charge. The only dramatic moment was when the clerk of the court said, "Will the defendant rise," and I started to get up out of my chair.

1984

From the story "My Father's Friends," published in *The New Yorker* and in *Billie Dyer and Other Stories*.

I FOUND MYSELF telling him about my guilty feelings at accepting my father's things, and he nodded and said, "Once when I was sitting in a jury box the judge said, 'Will the defendant rise,' and I caught myself just in time. If one isn't guilty of one thing one is certainly guilty of another is perhaps the only explanation for this kind of irrational behavior . . ."

1971

TUPELO'S SOUL AND his body have parted company. He was struck by a car crossing the road in front of our house in the country, last Friday night or Saturday morning, and Emmy was, alas, the one to find him. I heard the car drive into the driveway Saturday noon, and went for my coat so that I could help bring in the groceries and then heard a sound that horrified me—you know when you can't tell whether somebody is laughing or crying, and it always turns out that they are not laughing—she was standing in the kitchen and the children were holding her in their arms. I thought, at the time, that she had a passion for that animal, and I have since learned that I did too. And I took a box and went to get him. And when I saw him lying beside the road I thought for a moment—I said to myself, maybe it is some other cat, and then I saw that coon's tail. And the jaws spread wide. I wouldn't let anybody come near him, but Brookie brought me a pair of her much patched and mended overalls, and then a velvet bow, and then a little carved wooden bird. And with that, and wrapped in that, he lies under the frozen ground, by the playhouse in the backyard. But oh the tears.

There is no such thing as an ordinary cat but he was the most extraordinary cat I have ever known. So strong and healthy and brave and independent and humorous. When you picked him up it was like picking up physical perfection, and the lovely indescribable smell when you bury your face in his fur. He would let Emmy hold him, and Brookie, but he never stayed in my arms more than a minute. But on the other hand, when I was reading on the couch in the living room, he would leap up and settle there beside me and lick my fingers. He talked. All the time. He woke Emmy up one morning saying, "Merle?" He left his personality everywhere. The putting away of the toys, the velvet catnip mouse Emmy had made him, the traveling box, the kitty litter, the cat food, by red-eyed people. I don't seem to have any wisdom to bring to it, only grief.

1973

I HAD NO sooner received the new life of Virginia Woolf into my hands, last Monday, and agreed to write a review of it, remarking to the editor, "I'll drop everything to do it," but it sometimes take months, then I had a telephone call from my older brother and found myself on my way to Illinois to a funeral. My stepmother, who was 84, and had been ill a long time. She was a Catholic, and the strangest of the many strange things that happened to me was that during the funeral mass the relative who was sitting next to me, my stepmother's sister-in-law, whispered, "We take communion now. We go out this way,"—indicating the left side of the pew. Unable to believe my ears I said, "What?" and she repeated the same words, and when she got up I got up and stood in front of the altar and had a wafer put on my tongue.

The night I arrived, going up the walk to the front porch of the funeral home, as it is euphemistically called in the United States, though I don't know that "parlor" is much of an improvement, I was stopped by a series of old acquaintances, and in the third cluster of them was a very bent old woman with an exquisite profile, who when they told her who I was exclaimed "Billy!" and kissed the tips of my fingers. I knew her only slightly when I was growing up and I can only conclude that, on the razor's edge between living and dying herself, she had come to regard everything and everybody as beautiful and miraculous. As indeed they are.

1976

On beginning *So Long, See You Tomorrow.*

THIS IS THE seventh morning in a row that I have sat down to work on a novella about some farm people in Illinois in the Twenties. The fact that I seldom set foot on a farm in my childhood, though my father owned one, somewhat impedes me.

Some weeks later.

AS FOR THE novella, I have finally admitted to myself that it is that and not a short story . . .

After several months.

WHEN WE WERE in Wellfleet[4] I lay awake one night thinking about the novella and suddenly everything began to fall into place. I saw with excitement just how it should be, and sentences poured into my mind all night, nothing in my whole life was irrelevant, and in the morning when I got up and dressed I was exhausted, could remember nothing I had thought all night, was depressed, and felt I had been the victim of an illusion, and that I now knew what it was like to be a manic depressive in a manic phase. And did not even try to write for the next three

---

4   For a number of years, the Maxwells rented a house in the summer in Wellfleet, Massachusetts, on Cape Cod.

days. Writing has to be done on one's hands and knees, I told myself, and continued to plod along. But gradually it has been borne in on me that what I thought that night was correct after all, although just a little too excited to be manageable. I don't know how long it will turn out to be: something under 200 pages, I think. If I could draw a picture of it, it would look like this:

Turned sideways it is a woman.

Perhaps a year later.

WE GOT TO the country at last on Saturday, with Brookie, who immediately lit the oven and started making cookies. She had brought with her a quantity of hearts, roses, kittens, dogs, and children, circa 1912, to make valentines out of. The living room was awash with sentiment. It was lovely outside, but cold. And Sunday afternoon we came into town with a snowstorm at our heels. It snowed all night and is expected to snow all day and tonight, with an accumulation of twelve inches, by tomorrow morning. Which makes our trip to Washington D.C. uncertain. Even if LaGuardia Airport is open, will there be taxis? We have, with some friends, an appointment with the curator of Oriental Art at the Freer gallery. If Fortune favors us, we shall be unrolling scrolls of Sung, Ming, etc. dynasties. Otherwise I shall be sitting here in my bathrobe and pasting paragraphs about my farmers . . .

Undated

> *So Long, See You Tomorrow* was originally called
> "The Palace at 4 A.M.," after a piece of sculpture by
> Alberto Giacometti that is in The Museum of Mod-
> ern Art and that figures in the text. Howard Moss,
> the poetry editor of *The New Yorker*, had used the
> title for a play. Maxwell wrote him:

Dear Howard:

I have finished a short novel which Shawn has taken
for *The New Yorker* and Knopf is bringing out as a book
in January. The attached sheet, which I wrote for Judith
Jones,[5] will give you an idea of what it is about. The act
of violence referred to in the next to last paragraph is a
murder. In going over the manuscript with Roger[6] I have
just learned something I didn't know, or if I ever knew,
had forgotten: that you have a verse play with the same
title. I don't know what to do but throw myself on your
generosity. In the beginning of the novel there is a quite
necessary description of the Giacometti sculpture, and a
page and a half quotation from him about how it came
into being. At the end the palace becomes the focal point
of the action. With any other title I am fairly certain the
whole thing won't come off. Would I be doing you a serious injury if I kept it?

---

5 Maxwell's editor at Knopf.
6 Roger Angell, the editor at *The New Yorker* who handled the novel.

Undated

I OPENED "THE Peloponnesian War" last night (we were
going out for dinner and I had finished dressing before
Emmy) and read ". . . the elder men of the rich families who had these luxurious tastes only recently gave up
wearing linen undergarments and tying their hair behind their heads in a knot fastened with a clasp of golden
grasshoppers: the same fashion spread to their kinsmen
in Ionia, and lasted there among the old men for some
time." So that's what antiquity was like.

Undated

AS WE WERE leaving the country, I realized we had forgot
the dog's leash and went back, checked the front door to
see if it could blow open, left the keys in the lock, and off
we drove to town. For years Emmy has carried a second
set in her purse and two weeks ago the thought of drag-
ging all this needless weight prompted her to take them
out. I wasn't worried because I knew the superintendent
of our building had another set. He was off drinking beer,
and the keys on our hook in his apartment were from
before the lock was changed. It took two hours and a half,
a great deal of telephoning locksmiths, and $36 to get us
into our own home. Fortunately Emmy had made sand-
wiches of dark bread and the meat from the pot-au-feu
and the next-door neighbor was home, so we sat and ate
supper in her living room. The locksmith, when he came,

was a boy built on the lines of a lead pencil, and as dirty as a chimney sweep, and he had, judging by the marks on his face, been in a fight the night before. The lock turned out to be pickproof and had to be driven out with hammering, and I was glad it was not my hand that held the chisel. "Does this happen often on Sundays?" I asked when he was finished. "All day long," he said. "Seven days a week. Is this the first time it has happened to you?" "Yes," I said and then he said thoughtfully, "I don't suppose we would've met otherwise." Breaking my heart, though not for the first time.

The Room Outside
The New Yorker, 1998

THE HOUSE ON Ninth Street, where I lived as a child, had eleven-foot ceilings, and the downstairs rooms opened out of each other and were hard to heat. In late October, with the coal bill much on his mind, my father went from room to room downstairs stuffing toilet paper in the cracks between the windows and the window frames. Storm windows would have been better but they were unknown in our part of the country in the early decades of this century. There was a fireplace in the living room and another in the room we called the library, and when anyone tried to start a fire in either of them puffs of smoke would blow out into the room. The chimneys do not draw well when they are cold, and from the window seat in the library I watch as my father arranges paper

and kindling properly between the andirons, and then
the logs, and puts a match to the paper and stands holding an opened-out page of the Lincoln *Evening Courier*
across the upper part of the opening and waits patiently
for the air to start going up the chimney instead of out
into the room. If I pull the curtain around me and look
out into the winter night, I see the house next door, the
fence that divides our yard from the neighbors', a tree
trunk, sometimes the moon. If I let the curtain fall back
what I see is a reflection of the room I am in, superimposed on what is really out there. When the newspaper
catches on fire and vanishes up the flue (because it has
now begun to draw properly), I see that, too, reflected in
the windowpane.

*

IN THE WINTER of 1931 I have taken the train from Boston to Providence to spend the day with Cletus Oakley
and his wife. I am a graduate student at Harvard and
he is teaching at Brown. When I was a freshman at the
University of Illinois he made it impossible for me not
to understand differential and integral calculus. Now, in
his car, we drive to someplace near Pomfret, Connecticut, where the snow lies across the countryside in deep
drift. He has brought snow shoes for the three of us. I
have never had snowshoes on before and find it difficult
to keep from stepping on my own feet. We talk as we
walk and sometimes I trip and fall and Cletus helps me
up. The sun is shining out of a cobalt-blue sky and the
air is so dry that breathing it is a pleasure. (Why did I

never see them again when I liked them so much? How could I have been so stupid as to leave everything, including friendships, to chance?) When the light begins to fail, Cletus drives us to an eighteenth-century house, and there an old woman gives us tea and hot biscuits and honey. We are happy because of the fresh air and exercise, and she is happy because the spring garden catalogs have come.

✳

WHEN I WAS in my middle twenties I spent a winter on a farm in southern Wisconsin. There it was much colder than it was in Illinois, where, with the wind coming down off Lake Michigan, God knows it is cold enough. Bales of hay were banked all around the foundations of the farmhouse, which was heated by two sheet-iron wood-burning stoves, one upstairs and one downstairs in the room next to my small bedroom. And, of course, the cookstove in the kitchen. In the morning when I woke I sometimes saw a broadband of yellow light in the sky that I have never seen anywhere else, and before I could wash my face I often had to break a thin glaze of ice in the water pitcher on my dresser. The window had to be propped open, by a wooden spool in ordinary weather, a smaller spool if the temperature was twenty below, and if it was colder than that I didn't open the window at all. It was up to me to see that the woodbox in the kitchen was never empty and fill the reservoir on the side of the stove. The air was usually so dry that you could run out of the house in your shirtsleeves and fill a bucket of water at the pump but you couldn't touch the pump handle with your bare hands. I also had to keep a patch of ground bare and sprinkled with corn for the quail. If it rained when the temperature was hovering around thirty-two degrees their feathers froze and they couldn't fly into the shelter of the woods.

Eventually there was so much snow on the roads that the snow plow couldn't get through and we were snow-bound. One evening after supper the telephone rang and it was a neighbor saying that the mailman had got as far as the Four Corners, where our mailbox was. I put on extra-heavy underwear and, bundled to the eyes in sweaters and woolen scarves, I started to ski to the Four Corners. The snow drifts were higher than the horse-and-rider fences, obliterating the divisions between the fields, and I saw what nobody in the family and none of the neighboring farmers had ever seen: a pack of wild dogs running in a circle in the bright moonlight.

*

MY WIFE AND I are planning to spend the first Christmas of our married life in Oregon with her mother and father. We have been living in a small, one-story house in northern Westchester County. It started to snow at dusk the evening before our departure and it has snowed all night. The view from the kitchen window is cribbed from John Greenleaf Whittier. The town snowplows have kept our road open and a taxi delivers us at Harmon station in plenty of time, but for the last hour no trains have come in to or left the station. The ticket agent is noncommittal.

We wait and wait, consult the station clock, count our luggage. Privately I entertain the possibility that we will spend this Christmas at home. At that moment, far down the tracks to the south, there is a light. "The Twentieth Century Limited to Chicago arriving on Track Four!" the ticket agent announces over the public-address system, and in no time at all we are in our snug compartment looking out at the snow falling on the Hudson River. We are off. We have got away. Upstate New York, Pennsylvania, Ohio, and Indiana are like a long, uninterrupted white thought. In Chicago the slush is ankle deep. Then we pick up the thought where we left off. It is winter all the way across the Great Plains and the Rocky Mountains, but in Portland there is no snow on the ground and the camellias are in bloom.

✳

SEVERAL FAMILIES HAVE lived in the house on Ninth Street since my father sold it and some of them loved it as much as I did. They also made changes. Out of kindness, people—sometimes acquaintances, sometimes strangers—send me snapshots of the exterior from the front or the side. Our trees have died of old age or the elm blight and been replaced by others, but why the shutters, and what in Heaven's name happened to the porch railing? Nothing is right that isn't the way I remember it, and I drop the snapshots in the wastebasket. That room outside, superimposed on the snow: the reflection of the lamp, the table and the chair where my mother likes to sit when she sews, the white bookcase, the Oriental rugs, the man standing at the fireplace and the little boy peering out at the night—the image that was nothing more than a trick of the window glass—is indestructible.

ACKNOWLEDGMENTS

I am grateful to Kate Maxwell and Ellis Dolin Maxwell, William Maxwell's grandson, for their permission and support. And above all to Joshua Bodwell whose idea for a book this was. —A. W.

William Maxwell was born in Lincoln, Illinois, in 1908. He studied at the University of Illinois at Urbana-Champaign, and after earning a master's at Harvard, returned there to teach freshman composition before turning to writing. He published six novels, four collections of short fiction, an autobiographical memoir, a collection of literary essays and reviews, and two books for children. Maxwell served as a fiction editor at *The New Yorker* from 1936 to 1975. He received the Brandeis Creative Arts Award and Medal and, for *So Long, See You Tomorrow*, the National Book Award and the Howells Medal of the American Academy of Arts and Letters. He died in 2000 at the age of ninety-one.

Alec Wilkinson began writing for *The New Yorker* in 1980. Before that he was a policeman, and before that he was a rock-and-roll musician. He has published eleven books—including three memoirs, two collections of essays, two biographical portraits, and two pieces of reporting. His honors include a Guggenheim Fellowship, a Lyndhurst Prize, and a Robert F. Kennedy Book Award. He lives with his wife and son in New York City. His book about William Maxwell is called *My Mentor*.

A NOTE ON THE TYPE

The Writer as Illusionist has been set in Caslon. This modern version is based on the early-eighteenth-century roman designs of British printer William Caslon I, whose typefaces were so popular that they were employed for the first setting of the Declaration of Independence, in 1776. Eric Gill's humanist typeface Gill Sans, from 1928, has been used for display.

Book Design & Composition by Tammy Ackerman

GODINE NONPAREIL
Celebrating the joy of discovery with books bound to be classics.

Godine's Nonpareil paperback series features essential works by great authors—from stand-alone books of nonfiction and fiction to collections of essays, stories, interviews, and letters—introduced by celebrated contemporary voices who have deep connections to the featured authors and their trove of work.

ANN BEATTIE More to Say: Essays & Appreciations
Selected and Introduced by the author

GUY DAVENPORT The Geography of the Imagination: Forty Essays
Introduction by John Jeremiah Sullivan

ANDRE DUBUS The Lieutenant: A Novel
Afterword by Andre Dubus III

MAVIS GALLANT Paris Notebooks: Essays & Reviews
Foreword by Hermione Lee

WILLIAM MAXWELL The Writer as Illusionist: Uncollected & Unpublished Work
Selected and Introduced by Alec Wilkinson

JAMES ALAN McPHERSON On Becoming an American Writer: Nonfiction & Essays
Selected and Introduced by Anthony Walton

BHARATI MUKHERJEE Darkness: Stories
Introduction by the author and Afterword by Clark Blaise

ADELE CROCKETT ROBERTSON The Orchard: A Memoir
Foreword by Betsy Robertson Cramer and Afterword by Jane Brox

ALISON ROSE Better Than Sane: Tales from a Dangling Girl
Introduction by Porochista Khakpour

ALEC WILKINSON Midnights: A Year with the Wellfleet Police
Foreword by William Maxwell and Afterword by the author

MONICA WOOD Any Bitter Thing: A Novel
Introduction by Cathie Pelletier

Just as writing,

. But there is someting else that is not

ould have been merely a visual impression has the quality of an

emotional experience. Of a kind of disaster. Why? Why should this

visual impression, which you and I and everybody who has ever gone

on a train journey can recognize, have such aweight of sadness?

Something must have happened to him, he say to ourselves, and this

stage of train-sickness

Just what the writer meant us to think.

We have arrived at the

Let us get on with the journey: ⋏

Let us go on with the journey:

attempt 6

more sympathy and understanding than I gave him

Of the folded leaf, the published version, I find, six months

fter publication, that I have nothing whatever to say. It is done, *meant to probably continue*

s well as I knew how to do it, at the time, ~~though~~ if I wrote it

one thing I would explain to Peter, who ~~reads and deserves it~~, and I could explain and

ow, it would perhaps be entirely different, and the reviewers *better*

a synth version

~~d~~ If I wrote it five years from now, it would again be different *"The Folded Leaf"*

from the version I ~~would~~ *might* ~~one~~ to do now. ~~I~~ is that kind of novel.

Whenever I have an occasion *to go to The attic I see now*

But when I get the stepladder out and pullmyself through the tra

dpor of the attic, at home, and go in search of a glass bowl for

out a fe...

my wife, ~~or a roll of oilcloth~~, and happen to glance at a certain

corner, ~~there I see~~, in a box, a pile of yellow second paper roughl

consists of

~~ourteen~~ inches high. It represents the first, second, and third

The Folded Leaf.

complete versions, ~~as well as stray chapters~~, unfinished paragraph
made in the heat of what seemed like inspiration ~~An~~

and outlines scribbled in ~~pencil~~ and never looked at again. There

had not

~~were also~~ a good many pages ~~that~~ found there way directly into th

fireplace. But in such a stack, it alsways seems, there ought to

be usable material, for stories perhaps, or for another novel. T...

practically speaking

...for a moent, I turn away, knowing that there is nothing. but

...ublished work of fiction.

by once